GRAIL FOR SALE

Gerald Hammond

This first world edition published in Great Britain 2002 by
SEVERN HOUSE PUBLISHERS LTD of
9–15 High Street, Sutton, Surrey SM1 1DF.
This first world edition published in the USA 2002 by
SEVERN HOUSE PUBLISHERS INC of
595 Madison Avenue, New York, N.Y. 10022.

British Library Cataloguing in Publication Data

Hammond, Gerald, 1926–
    Grail for sale
    1. Antiques business – Scotland – Fiction
    2. Detective and mystery stories
    I. Title
    823.9'14 [F]

ISBN 0-7278-5807-6

Typeset by Palimpsest Book Production Ltd.,
Polmont, Stirlingshire, Scotland.
Printed and bound in Great Britain by
MPG Books Ltd., Bodmin, Cornwall.

This story, along with the characters therein, is imaginary. However, the theory concerning the nature of the Grail originated, I believe, with Noel Currer-Briggs and I drew some of the material from his book *The Shroud And The Grail*.

G.H.

One

The other car appeared suddenly at him out of the rain. He thought for a frantic instant that it was being driven at him on the wrong side of the road, but then realized that it was facing away from him and had been halted, mostly on what poor substitute for a verge there was. He slowed further and had a good look as he went by. Somebody might want a lift to a garage or to be sent help. But the car, though it seemed undamaged, was deserted. The rain was heavy enough for the rebounding spray to conceal details but the car seemed to have an exhausted look. He was sure that if the visibility had been better he would have seen dents and rust. He nodded sympathetically. He knew all about motoring on a shoestring.

The very minor road in the Scottish Borders was running there through barren moorland and offered no havens to the casual visitor. He was unsurprised, therefore, after a mile or two, to come up behind a figure plodding miserably in the same direction. The figure was that of a young woman and she was leaning against the weight of a large bag or holdall. Jeremy's first reaction was that of the average unattached male, compounded of an impulse towards knight-errantry and a touch of male interest. A contrary thought was that

1

women had been known to seek lifts on lonely roads with the intention of extorting money under the threat of crying 'Rape!'

He slowed to a crawl beside the woman, then stopped and wound his window down, trying to ignore the raindrops which were bouncing off the door. She was such a plain-looking girl with artificially curly hair in a wet tangle, peering at him with difficulty through spectacles which she had endeavoured to wipe dry with a well-used handkerchief, that he was sure no judge or jury would give credence to an allegation of rape.

'Can I give you a lift somewhere?' he asked.

Hazel Tripp looked critically at his blurred image. Men sometimes stopped to offer girls lifts with evil intentions. But this one did not look that sort and, as well as she could judge by his receding hairline and ragged beard, she would not have given much for his chances of overpowering her. Anyway, given the choice between ravishment and being left to squelch in disintegrating shoes and sodden clothes along a desolate road to nowhere . . . well, her decision, she told herself, might not be altogether a foregone conclusion.

'Where are you making for?'

'About ten miles along this road,' he said, 'but I'll put you on your way to wherever you're going. Do get in. Please.'

While she limped round the car, he wound up his window and brushed raindrops off the sleeve of his tweed jacket, only to have his other sleeve dampened as she dropped her bag into the rear space and settled into the only other seat. She really was very, very wet. He turned up the heater and the small sports car began to fill with steam. He wiped the inside of the windscreen with the back of his hand. 'Well?' he said. 'Where to? A garage?'

'I don't think so,' she said slowly. 'You passed my car back there? When it stopped, there was a noise under the bonnet like a knight in full armour falling off his horse and I don't have money for a major repair. Anyway, a mechanic told me that it was going to fail its next MOT on about fifty-two counts, and that's due in six weeks. It can stay where it is.' At first, he had been more interested in her words, but he was becoming aware of an accent, American or possibly Canadian.

'They'll charge you for removing it.'

'They'll have to find me first. I'll just have to hitchhike the rest of the way. I'm heading in the direction of Dumfries.'

Her voice was meant to sound confident but he could detect a tremor. 'This side of Dumfries?' he asked.

'Beyond Dumfries. I have a friend near Kirkcud-bright. I've come from Edinburgh.'

'You were going a bit out of your way, weren't you?'

'I went to Galashiels first. I was hoping to get a bed there but my other friend was away. I've used this road before as a sort of short cut.'

He sighed. She was on her uppers and on the scrounge for accommodation. Presumably she would have phoned ahead and discovered her friend's absence except for a fear of being met with excuses. He could hardly push her out into the rain, but he had no desire to go another trip of nearly a hundred miles each way in pouring rain. And his windscreen wipers were suspect, the blades overdue for renewal. They drove in silence for some minutes.

He slowed. They were arriving at the castle gates. 'I

live here,' he said. 'You'd better come in for a hot bath and change into dry clothes. You can wait until the rain stops.' *And no longer*, he added silently.

'If it ever does stop,' she said.

He drew up in the road, opposite the open gates. She was weighing him up out of the corner of her eye. 'All you have to do when we get inside,' he said, 'is to pick up the phone and call your mother or a friend and tell them that you're at Tinnisbeck Castle with me, Jeremy Carpenter. That way I can hardly bury you in the garden or sell you to the white slavers. It's that or start walking again.'

The name Tinnisbeck Castle was carved into one of the stone pillars supporting the ornate but slightly rusty gates. 'I'm Hazel Tripp,' she said. It was an apology as well as an introduction.

The gravel was too compact and weed-strewn to crunch under the wheels. They drove beneath a tunnel of trees, leafless in February, then emerged and climbed for a quarter of a mile through moorland. Beyond the last rise, the castle squatted defensively within a margin of garden and lawn, all, as well as she could see in the failing light, overgrown. The castle was mostly comprised of a single massive tower. The overall impression, seen through the rain, was gloomy and she remembered words from *King Lear*. *Childe Rowland to the dark tower came.* The phrase had always seemed to her to be doom-laden yet somehow improbable, but now it suddenly seemed wholly apt. The castle was a mixture, she judged, of the very old and the fairly old, with the addition, probably during the reign of Victoria, of enlarged windows and, she hoped, other amenities. She had no fancy for a hip-bath in front of an open

4

fire. The building probably commanded a panoramic view across country, but in the dwindling visibility it was impossible to tell.

He parked on a circle of gravel close to a big main door. So, she decided, at least he wasn't the butler. But there were no lights shining out to greet the returning master.

'No point in getting any wetter,' Jeremy said. 'Let's just do this my way.' He withdrew a huge key from the glove compartment and reached behind the seat to draw a large golf umbrella from the jumble of coats and sticks beneath her holdall. The rain was coming down as heavily as ever. He pushed his door open an inch or two and erected the umbrella quickly, then climbed out under its shelter. He walked round the car. 'Now you bring your bag out,' he suggested.

She joined him under the umbrella. 'Thanks. Not that I could have got much wetter.'

'But I could. Now you hold the umbrella while I get my week's shopping out of the boot.'

Hazel held the umbrella while he collected a card-board carton and pushed the boot lid down with his elbow. They moved clumsily side by side up three steps to the recess for the door, where at least they were partially sheltered from the rain. Jeremy managed to raise one knee to support the carton while he wrestled with the enormous key. It was a tricky operation, honed, she decided, by years of practice. He had to lean against the heavy door, which must have been of solid oak and four inches thick, to push it open.

The entrance hall was roofed by a single stone cross-vault, pierced by a winding staircase. It was large, gloomy, bare, echoing and absolutely freezing

5

cold. She was about to say that she would be warmer out in the rain when her host led her to a door and stood aside for her to open it. It opened onto a large and blessedly warm kitchen.

Her companion deposited the box on a large, scrubbed table. She noticed that the shopping was a typically male collection of convenience foods and luxury items, with UHT milk and only two six-packs of beer. The warmth was emanating from a large range and she stood and dripped while he gave it a quick riddle and refuelled it from a coke-scoop. 'This provides hot water,' he said, 'but I'm afraid it doesn't heat more than the kitchen, so I tend to live in here by day. There's a bathroom almost next door. Have a hot bath and change into dry clothes and you'll feel better. Use as much water as you like. I'll have my bath later.'

She had begun delving into her holdall. 'All my stuff seems to fall somewhere between damp and soggy,' she said. 'Can you lend me a dressing-gown or something while I air some clothes?'

'One thing I do have is a good airing cupboard,' he said. 'Hang on a moment.' He vanished through another door and she heard a tap running. She looked around the kitchen, which was as vast in scale as the rest of the place and as shabby and utilitarian but functional. It had been recently and brightly gloss-painted, but without much care given to the preparation of surfaces, so that a myriad old dents and scratches showed through. The Welsh-type dresser had been knocked together by an unskilled craftsman and was fit for firewood but among the ill-assorted crockery it supported were one or two pieces of good Delft and one of Wedgwood. A second table in a corner supported a large computer and some papers. It was flanked by stack upon stack of books and more papers. A television set stood on a stool. The chairs were Windsor and were definitely good even if they made no concessions to luxurious living.

Jeremy came back in a minute or two. 'There are some clothes and a towel on the rail,' he said. 'The bathroom's the second door on the left. Pass me out what you're wearing and I'll hang it to dry in front of the range.'

She put his age at about thirty or perhaps a little over, so there should be nothing among her underwear to surprise him. 'Thanks.'

She draped her sodden coat over one of the Windsor chairs. When she had taken it off it seemed impossibly heavy. She went through into what had obviously once been the servants' quarters. The bathroom was as humid as the day outside, but this was not cold rain but lovely, comforting steam. She adjusted the temperature of the water, threw her clothes out into the passage and settled in to soak the chill out of her small body.

A little later, he knocked on the door. 'Do you mind if I empty your bag and hang up the rest of your things?'

'If you're that kind and helpful, go ahead.'

The toiletries were all definitely male. She washed her hair with a masculine shampoo. The towels were rough but at least they were warm and dry. Instead of a robe he had left a selection of his own clothes for her. So there was no other woman in the house.

She returned to the kitchen, well aware that she must be a comical figure; but she was quite without vanity and had never worried much about her personal appearance. Her hair was wrapped in a hand-towel and she was wearing a checked shirt, a pair of jeans with the cuffs turned up and too-large carpet-slippers. For underwear she had only a pair of Y-fronts which were certain to slip down. But the loaned clothes were all bone dry and deliciously warm. She found that her holdall had been emptied and her clothes were arranged carefully on a large clothes-horse beside the range. Two magazines from her holdall were laid out open to dry on a shelf.

Her host seemed to have changed his more obvious garments and tidied himself. He looked quite respectable with his hair brushed. Surely his beard had been trimmed and tidied, transforming him from an unkempt man of the woods into a civilized and halfway dapper human being? He was attending to several pans on the top of the range.

'I hope you like scampi,' he said. 'I wasn't expecting a guest.'

'I love scampi.'

'Shall we have some wine with it? I have the run of my grandfather's cellar.'

So, unless he was a drink-driver, he was not going to offer her a run to Kirkcudbright that evening. It would have been too much to expect. Was he going to push her out into the rain? At least she seemed to be getting a meal out of it.

'A glass of wine would go down well,' she said cautiously.

He nodded. 'White, I suppose, with scampi.' He looked at her uncertainly. 'I'm afraid I don't have a hair-drier. Would you like to manage over one end of the range?'

As a compromise, she sat on the floor with her back

near the open fire-door and brushed out her dark hair as it dried. Frowning at herself in a small hand-mirror, she said, 'I should get my money back on this home perm. I've gone straight again.'

He looked at her critically. She had delicate features with large, brown eyes and full lips. 'Frizzy hair didn't suit you anyway,' he said at last. 'You still have natural waves.'

She noted his remark without commenting, but she left her spectacles on the shelf beside her magazines. She seldom needed them, but she had worn them in the rain for safe carrying. She had had a spectacle case but lost it months earlier.

A little later, they sat down to a generous meal. She suspected that they were making a serious inroad into what should have been his week's rations, but she had missed lunch and she was ravenous. He had produced a half-bottle of a respectable wine. So he did not intend to ply her with alcohol.

When appetite was at least partly satisfied she said, to make conversation, 'So it's your grandfather's house? Castle, I mean.'

He nodded and emptied his mouth. 'One of the few castles around these parts that the Earl of Sussex didn't destroy after the "Rebellion of the Bankrupt Earls". He tried, but the keep held out against him and he only managed to burn the rest of it, reducing the place to a more manageable size. I live here rent-free as a sort of caretaker tenant. The old chap lives in a nursing home in Carlisle and doesn't expect to come out again, ever. He's quite happy there,' Jeremy added quickly, 'or quite as happy as one can expect to be when life's slowly draining away, and I visit him as often as I can, usually once or twice a month.'

Hazel allowed him to refill her glass. 'And your parents?' she asked.

'Both drowned. Their yacht went down in a storm, somewhere off the Lofoten Islands.'

She flushed. 'I'm sorry. I wouldn't have asked . . .'

'It's all right. You weren't to know. And it was nearly fifteen years ago. The old chap's the only relative I know of. He finished my upbringing. I owe him a lot.'

There was a huskiness in his voice and she thought he was upset at having brought his secret emotions into the daylight. In search of a quick change of subject she said, 'It must cost the earth to heat a place this size.'

'It does,' he said grimly. He saw that her glass was still full and emptied the last of the half-bottle into his own. 'There's a solid-fuel boiler that heats the whole place but I can't afford to light it very often. So I just look on it as a necessity to keep the building from deteriorating. It's an upside-down situation. When we get what my mother would have called a "good drying day" and don't need the heating for comfort, I light the boiler, open a lot of windows and give the whole place a good airing.'

They did the washing-up together. She felt her clothes, which were already half dry. She made a small rearrangement so that a pair of panties was not so provocatively on show. The rain was still lashing down outside and rattling against the windows, so they settled near the range in the Windsor chairs which, with the addition of a couple of cushions, were surprisingly comfortable.

'It's none of my damn business,' she said, 'and you're welcome to tell me so, but what do you do for a living?'

He gave a small snort of laughter without seeming in the least amused. 'Or do I just sponge off my grandfather, you mean?'

'I didn't mean anything of the sort,' she said indignantly – and guiltily.

'Then perhaps you meant, why didn't I get a proper *job*? Live in a nice warm flat and let this place go to rack and ruin?'

'If you're going to put words into my mouth . . .'

She sounded hurt and he felt immediate compunction. She was his first female company, almost his first company, in months and he was losing the knack of conversation. She would be gone in the morning, but in the meantime there was no need to hurt her feelings.

'I shouldn't do that, should I? I'm sorry,' he said gently. 'Perhaps it's a habit of my profession. And I've been subjected to that sort of implied criticism rather often. I must learn to ride with it. You see, I'm a historian.' He had meant to leave it at that, but he saw that he had caught her interest so he went on, 'I give some lectures but most of my time goes into research and writing. Financially, it's a long-term prospect. If you write a standard textbook, it may stay in print for twenty or thirty years but the return's small at first. So a rent-free roof over the head is a blessing, but I don't take money from my grandfather. Quite the reverse. I spend two-thirds of the year trying to put by enough money so that I can spend the summer on field trips to libraries, museums, archaeological sites and anywhere else that I can gather something useful.' He paused and decided that he had made enough of an apology for snapping at her. 'Tell me about you. How do you come to be stranded in the rain, miles from anywhere and – am I right? – seeming rather footloose?'

'Footloose is right,' she said sadly. 'I have no roots anywhere now. I was born in Maine and brought up in the antiques world.'

'I guessed that from the magazines.'

She nodded. 'Antiques are big business in the States but we don't have them going back that far back. Most of what we have, you'd consider almost modern. So I decided to try my luck over here and learn a bit about where it all comes from.'

'So what went wrong?'

'Everything,' she said simply. 'I was working in one of those antique shops in the Royal Mile, renting a small flat and not putting anything away for my fare home. The original foolish virgin, not that I could lay claim to being one of those. The shop was bought out by that bastard McKennerty. I know now that he'd spotted some goodies we'd missed. He closed it down, sold the stock through the auction houses and the shop's a wine-bar now. I tried to hang on but there were no jobs going and I ran out of money. End of sad story.'

'That was tough,' he said. There was real sympathy in his voice. He stood for a moment and looked out of the window. 'The rain's letting up but you won't get far tonight. I've lit a fire in my bedroom and you can have that. I'll take a shakedown in here.'

Even if he had dry pillows and bedding in the airing cupboard, he would be unlikely to have an aired mattress. 'I never meant to put you out,' she said. She paused and studied him. He was slim for a man but well

12

proportioned. With his beard dried and brushed he was neat and she could see a kindly mouth to go with gentle eyes. His voice was educated – she had been in Britain long enough to recognize the shades of accent – and it had a timbre which pleased her. Significantly, he had befriended a stranger without making any demands.

There was one gesture which she could think of to repay his kindness. 'Stop me if I'm speaking out of turn,' she said suddenly, 'but you're a grown man and though I've not been exactly promiscuous I'm not a dewy-eyed innocent. You're a nice guy, you've been kind and a woman has needs too. We could share.'

He looked at her again. In the unsuitable clothes her figure, which was good, looked exotic and vaguely disturbing. 'I'd like that,' he said simply. 'You don't have to, you know.'

She came up with a smile which seemed to warm the air between them. 'I know I don't. I think I'd like to. Let's just see how we get along. If it doesn't work out, we can shake hands and part as friends. No embarrassment. OK?'

He led her through into a small but comfortable bedroom, cosy with firelight. They kissed and she was relieved to find his beard clean, dry, soft and sweet-smelling. From the first moment of their foreplay, each was sure that it was going to be good; but their pleasure was almost spoiled when they realized that they had not a single prophylactic between them.

'That's it, then,' she said. 'I trust you as far as I'll trust any man, but I'm not going to risk being made pregnant by a man I only met today. Unless . . .'

'Unless?'

'Unless you like what I like. I know I'm clean and I'm sure that you are.'

He did like what she liked, a sweet and more delicate alternative to the mating act.

A little later, he raised his head. 'You never made that phone call,' he said. 'Anything could be happening to you.'

She had to laugh through her nose.

Two

Hazel awoke slowly and luxuriously, alone in a strange bed. Sunshine, filtered through floral curtains, gave the small bedroom a woodland gloom. The fire was out but the heavy chimney had held the heat and the room was still warm.

Her hairbrush was probably still in the kitchen so she made use of Jeremy's, examining it carefully afterwards to be sure that she had not left any of her own hairs on it. She had slept nude, so she put on his shirt again and padded barefoot through to the kitchen, bracing herself for *Thank you and goodbye*. If he offered her money, she decided, she would be insulted but she would have to accept it. Perhaps she had been mad to give herself so easily, but her pleasure had been at least as great as his and she could take to the road again in the comfort of dry clothes and a day which, she saw when she pulled back the curtains, had turned genuinely fine and was not just a reflection of her own bodily contentment.

There was an almost painfully beautiful smell of coffee. Lit by the sun, the kitchen had a new aspect, cheerful instead of grimly functional. Her clothes were still warming by the range. Her host was sitting in a typist's chair at the computer. When he heard her arrive, he careful finished his paragraph, saved his work on the

15

disk drive and on a floppy and then got up. 'There's coffee in the pot,' he said, pointing, 'or the kettle's hot if you'd like tea. Proper tea, not American herbal stuff. Cereal in the packets, bread in the bin, toaster over there, milk in the fridge and if you like something cooked I'll do it for you.'

He came to a halt in front of her and kissed her suddenly, to her surprise. His beard had been washed again.

'Cereal, coffee and toast suits me,' she said. 'Don't let me hold you back if you want to get on.'

'I've always been an early riser,' he said, 'and I can only write in a series of short bursts. I've done enough for the moment. It's always good to stop while it's going well. It makes it easier to get going again.'

After yesterday's soaking, a night of sex and a long sleep, she was ravenous. He watched her, still wearing only his shirt, as she served herself and then sat down opposite her. While he had company, he felt the need to make the most of it. He recalled a topic from the previous evening. 'You mentioned the name McKennerty last night,' he said. 'Would that be Gordon McKennerty? A tubby man with a heavily modelled face, high colour and a rather haughty manner. Lives somewhere in Edinburgh.'

While she emptied her mouth she was nodding. 'Right,' she said. 'I'd have said domineering rather than haughty, but we're talking about the same guy. He lives in one of the big houses in Ravelstone Dykes or somewhere like that, in back of the zoo.'

'Why did you call him a bastard? Just because he bought out your employer?'

This time, she shook her head. 'He's famous for it,'

she said. 'Being a bastard, I mean. Dealers need to be tough, but he's ruthless.'

'I didn't know that he was a dealer. I thought he was just a well-heeled collector.'

She finished her cereal before replying. Her toast had popped up and he fetched it and put a jar of marmalade in front of her.

'Thanks. Well-heeled, yes. Collector, maybe. Collector of money, more like. Bastard, definitely. He doesn't have a shop, he just has a knack of spotting unrecognized treasures. He does private deals, big-time, from that house of his, to support a whale of a lifestyle. Around now, he's usually away to the South of France until spring and God knows what he gets up to there, but the rest of the year, it's parties with wines like you and I will never afford and good-time girls provided for friends and clients. He'll give his rich buddies a square deal, but anyone else he eats for breakfast.' She lowered her voice. 'They say that whatever you want, he can find it.'

'Stealing to order, you think?' She nodded. He waited until she had finished her first slice of toast and was buttering another. 'He gave me a fair enough deal on a bronze figurine,' he said. 'My own, not my grandfather's. It was the last of the few things that came down to me from my parents. He showed me the price in *Miller's Guide* and gave me slightly more.'

'Doesn't sound like the same guy. What year was the *Guide*?'

'It was current. I looked. I'm not that simple.'

'Maybe not. What sort of figurine?'

'It was a figure of a dancing girl. The name *Belmont* was cast into the base in a geometric sort of script, if

17

that's any help. The *Guide* said eight-fifty and he gave me nine hundred.'

'Did it say *Solange* on the other side?'

'Yes.'

'How big was it?'

He held his hand about half a metre above the table-top.

She finished her toast in silence, drank her coffee and then carried her few dishes to the sink. 'I don't like having to tell you this,' she said over her shoulder, 'but just in case you want to sell something else, you'd better know. You were had. Evangeline Belmont was one of the stars of the Art Nouveau. You seldom hear her name – she worked a lot with Charles Rennie Macintosh and she was very much in his shadow – but her own works are becoming highly collectable. *Solange* was one of the last things she did before she died. Her first modelling of it was eighteen inches high, but that was too big for most people's rooms and she copied it again, seven inches tall, and that one was cast a whole lot of times. Somehow it didn't have quite the spirit of the original. Even so, that's the one that goes for around eight-fifty and that's what he showed you in the *Guide*. Very few were made of the larger one. There have been copies made, casts from one of the originals, but they don't come out too good, they don't have the patina and anyway the measurements give them away. They come out a mite smaller than the original because the metal contracts in the casting.'

She finished drying her few dishes and took down her magazines from the shelf. 'The sale was reported. I think it's in one of these . . . Yes, here we are. That's your figurine?'

The photograph brought it back to him. It showed the figure of a dancing girl, nude. The commonplace subject was somehow imbued with joy, humour and a zest for life. The price paid at auction was quoted. He looked and looked again.

'Holy fer-funning cheese!'

'It's all right. You can swear if you want. You've paid for the privilege.'

He took several deep breaths. 'I don't have to swear aloud,' he said. 'I'm swearing like you wouldn't believe, inside my mind.' He walked quickly out of the kitchen.

There was an ironing board propped in a corner. She was tempted to ready her one passable dress but she sensed that it would be out of place in the countryside and might give the impression that she was angling to stay. She dressed quickly in a light jersey and jeans – not the ones with the fashionable rips and tears which she had worn the previous day. She sensed that the designer damage which, in the city, was part of the current scene would look to him as if the jeans had been salvaged from the scrapheap. Her only half-suitable shoes were her old trainers. She applied a touch of makeup from a small tin in her holdall.

Jeremy had made his exit along the passage where his bedroom and bathroom were to be found. A door at the far end was open to the sunshine. An inner door was slightly ajar and, peeping inside, she saw a large and ancient boiler which was emitting complacent noises and no little heat. Immediately outside, a lean-to roof sheltered a large pile of coke. Looking up, she saw that windows had been opened.

The air was cool but clean and fresh and she could feel the city fumes washing out of her lungs. She followed the terrace around the low kitchen wing and then the massive walls of the keep and found him sitting on a low wall near the main door, looking over a prospect that extended for ten miles or more. In the rain and the fading light, she had not appreciated how the ground had been rising, but now she could see that the modest garden soon became heather which gave way to farmland on the lower ground. The bottom of the valley was wooded. The roofs of houses showed through the bare trees and she could see a river. Then the hills and heather began again.

He seemed to be absorbed and she decided to leave him to his bitterness, but he heard her footsteps, turned and held out a hand to her. The look that they exchanged contained both warmth and reserve. They had been intimate without getting to know each other, so that neither was sure of the new relationship. She put her hand on the wall. It had been warming ever since dawn in a rare winter sun. She took a seat beside him.

'A few days like this wouldn't have been out of place last summer,' he said.

'Yes. Or no. Whatever.'

They sat for a minute in companionable silence.

'You were right,' he said. 'McKennerty's a bastard. You had just the word for him.'

'I'm sorry I told you now. You were contented with what you got. Truth's fine, but not if somebody's happier without it.'

He was silent, apparently unheeding. 'That money would have made all the difference,' he said at last. 'It costs the earth to keep my grandfather in his retirement nursing home. I càn't bring myself to tell the old chap that his money's running out. I'm trying to keep this place up, keep him going and still support my studies and it can't be done for much longer. I couldn't do it at all without writing historical documentaries for television, but it's all time taken away from my real work. I have my grandfather's power of attorney. I could sell the place but . . .'

'But it means too much to you,' she said, reading his voice.

'I spent a lot of my youth here. It's my home. I'm his only living relative closer than second cousins in South Africa, so I suppose the place comes to me – if he hasn't willed it to the National Trust, which he's threatened more than once to do when he's lost patience with me. A good injection of cash would have kept me going on all fronts until I was better established.'

'Has it always been in your family?'

'Since the year dot. Not always in the same names – titles have come and gone and sometimes it's come down through the female line.'

She turned around to let the sun warm her back and to look up at the building. In the sunshine it was an old and battered but friendly place, solid but welcoming. She recalled her father once saying that you should never buy a house without first seeing it in the rain. 'I can't blame you for loving it,' she said. 'It's like some faces. There's nothing special about the bits but it all adds together to make something special. My face is just the opposite,' she added. 'There's nothing wrong with my eyes or my nose or my mouth or my chin, but they don't add up to anything much.'

They were side by side but facing in opposite directions, so that it was easy for him to study her profile from close range. She had good eyes, brown with flecks of green. Her nose was straight and slightly tip-tilted. Her mouth was generous. The overall effect was characterful and rather charming. 'Rubbish,' he said. She sat patiently while he considered her carefully. 'You do have good features. If you had a more flattering hairstyle, you could be attractive and more. Your eyes are beautiful. What happened to your glasses?'

'I only need them for close-up work. I was wearing them yesterday because they were safer on my nose than in my pocket.'

'Well, there's nothing wrong with the way your bits are put together, now that I see you in a proper light and with your hair in waves instead of that silly frizz which was much too young for you anyway. What ever put such a daft idea into your head?'

Hazel hesitated between feeling indignant and flattered and ended up amused. 'I suppose it was my father. He always called me "Funny-face" and I suppose I came to believe it.'

'And nobody ever told you how nice you can look?'

'If they did, I thought it was just the thing people say. It isn't just that with you?'

She waited anxiously for his answer.

'Why would I flatter you?' he asked. 'I don't have to lie to get you into my bed, you've already been there. And when you smile like that, you're beautiful.'

She would have liked to prolong the subject a little further but she felt suddenly shy. 'You've been very kind,' she said. 'But you won't want me intruding on you. I suppose I'd better be moving along.'

'Where to?'

'I don't know. I'll find somewhere.'

'Do you want to go?' He surprised himself by adding, 'You're welcome to stay here.'

'Would you like me to stay on?'

His eyebrows went up and she thought that he was half-smiling behind the beard. 'Of course I would. I didn't even expect to have to say it. We have a rapport and we were so good together . . . Don't you want to stay?'

She smiled again. 'Of course I do. It's like a gift from God. I hoped you'd say what you did.' The smile faded into anxiety. 'You needn't think I'd hang round your neck for ever; you'd only have to say that you wanted me to go and I'd go. I needn't be a burden to you. I don't have any money but I can cook. And I'm a great typist, if that's any help.'

He put his arms round her waist. 'I, for my part, am a rotten typist. I write everything out longhand and copy-type it when I've got it right, and even with a word-processing program in the computer it takes me for ever.'

'Your writing's quite legible, which makes a change. I looked.'

'A competent typist who can cook—'

'And give great sex?'

'—and give absolutely superlative sex—'

'I can shovel coke, too,' she said. 'And, if you like, I could look over your antiques. An old place like this, there's always valuables which nobody's ever thought much about.'

'The perfect woman.'

It was pleasant in the sun but she was beginning to

feel cold. He felt her shiver and let go so that they could stand up, but they walked back round the walls linked together again. 'If I'm taking over the catering,' she said, 'we can manage a better balanced diet than those junk foods you've been living on.'

'I never have the time or the skill to cook from scratch, so I let some food-preparation establishment do all the work. Take my car. I'd better give you a cheque. The post office in the village cashes them. The shop keeps fresh fruit and vegetables.'

'Is there a drugstore? What you call a chemist? There's something we need.'

He laughed joyously. 'There's a hairdresser behind the pub. They keep them there.'

'It won't bother you if I turn up in your car, cash your cheque and then buy condoms?'

He was still chuckling. 'Around here, everybody knows everybody's business inside a couple of days and they always think the worst. So we may as well let them know that we're being careful. My grandfather always insisted that the castle sets a good example.'

Two days later, the computer and printer had been transferred to another and smaller table which Jeremy brought up from a cellar. Hazel tidied her papers and switched off the printer. 'There we are. I've caught up with you.' She looked carefully at Jeremy, who was scratching his head with a pencil-point and scowling at the wall. 'You're aren't with it, are you?' she said.

Jeremy looked up abstractedly and shook his head. He had taken advantage of the space freed from the computer and printer to stack even more books on his table. 'That gives me a good kick forward. Without the need to copy-type my work I could have been making progress,' he said. 'But my mind keeps jumping back to what I could have done with that money. I could have paid for my grandfather's keep for a few months up front, put money by for a study trip and bought an absolute mountain of coke.'

'There's no point brooding about what might have been. Take your mind off it.' She leafed through the freshly printed pages. 'Or at least half off it. Are you sure of what you wrote about the Holy Grail?'

'About as sure as one can be of anything in history, when there are at least two versions of absolutely everything. Bear in mind that the earliest recorded legends about the Grail stem from three medieval troubadours. They may be founded on older and possibly factual legends or they may not. The legends certainly went on to become linked with the Arthurian legend and to descend into pure romantic fiction. What in particular?'

Hazel got up and crossed the kitchen and felt the percolator. It was still hot. 'Coffee time,' she said. 'In particular, what is or was the Grail?'

Jeremy stretched, stood up and moved to one of the Windsor chairs at the big table. 'Good question,' he said, 'but a long story. Why do you want to know?'

'I was brought up in the antiques business, remember. If it still existed it would undoubtedly be the most valuable antique in the world. The very word has come to mean the search for something infinitely precious.'

Jeremy gave a shout of laughter and was struck by how laughter-free his solitary life had been. 'You're thinking of going on a crusade of your own? You've got to be joking!'

Hazel smiled patiently. 'Perhaps. But I still want to know, and if I waited for your book to come out I still couldn't afford to buy it. So tell me.'

'All right.' Jeremy settled in his chair, looked at the ceiling and assumed the manner of the habitual lecturer. 'At various times, it has been supposed to be a secret and nothing substantial at all. It has also been believed to be vessels of various sizes, a receptacle for a severed head, a magic stone, an emerald or other precious stone from Lucifer's crown, a horn of plenty or the Cathar Treasure. But in the main, it has been inseparably linked with the Christian story. At one time it was reputed to consist of a series of changing images of Christ, but by late in the fifteenth century it had assumed the identity of the cup of the Last Supper.'

Hazel poured coffee from the percolator and came to sit down opposite him. 'But you don't believe that,' she said.

'No, I don't. The Grail's closely associated with the Shroud. It has most often been referred to as some sort of container, bearing traces of the blood and sweat of Christ. It was almost certainly the box which, until about the fourteenth century, contained the Shroud.'

'Wow!' Hazel said. 'And there's evidence for that?'

'Of a sort, if you look for it. Whole books have been written about it, both for and against. One line of argument is this. Most of the early icons bearing the supposedly authentic face of Christ show Him against a background of trellis-work. There's a quite simple explanation. Christ's initial in Greek, the letter Chi, appeared as our X; and X only needs the addition of a segment of a circle to be turned into the symbol of *ichthus*, the fish, the very early symbol of Christianity.

X also represents the crosses of St Andrew and St Patrick. Make a pattern of Xs and you have a trellis. That trellis pattern seems to have been adopted by medieval artists as portraying a special sort of sanctity. I know of two boxes in Nuremburg dating from the fourteenth century. One, a silver box with criss-cross strips of gold, holds the relics of St Sebald; the other, also with a criss-cross pattern, once contained the relics belonging to the Holy Roman Emperors.

'Now imagine a box, containing the Shroud and covered with such a symbolic pattern. It bears either a painting of the head of Christ as it appears on the Shroud, or possibly a glass insert so that the image of the head on the Shroud can be seen. This is precisely the subject copied by the early painters.

'The word Grail has been the subject of endless argument between scholars, but if you go back to the *Dictionary of Ancient and Medieval French*, you'll find that it gives the word *greil* or *greille*, translating it as a grille, trellis or lattice. Skeat's etymological dictionary tracks it through old French words meaning dishes of various shapes but also comes round to both a gridiron and a hurdle. Plenty of room for confusion.'

'That does sound sort of feasible,' Hazel said ruminatively. 'So what became of it?'

'That's another very long question. The history of the Shroud and its casket is fairly well documented until it came into the possession of the Templars after the fall of Constantinople in twelve ninety-three and it seems to have been taken to their *de facto* headquarters at Montpellier. About fifteen years later, the French king, Philip the Handsome, was in dire need of money and was casting greedy eyes at the Templars. Some scandals were fabricated or exaggerated to justify a wholesale arrest of the order. You may care to note that the principal accusation was of worshipping an idol or "head" – which very few people had actually seen.'

'And "head" could refer to . . . what you just described?'

'In my opinion, yes, it could. After the wholesale arrests in October of that year, the Shroud ended up in the possession of a long-serving member, Geoffrey de Charnay. De Charnay had German connections and the Shroud seems to have been sent to Germany for safekeeping.

'During the nearly fifty years that the Shroud spent in Germany before returning to France, it seems to have become separated from its original container. Certainly the box in which it was eventually presented to the Pope was more recent; but then, there's some question as to whether that Shroud was original. There may have been a substitution of both at around that time. A copy of the Shroud was said to have been destroyed during the French Revolution, but could that have been the real one? Is that why carbon-dating places the Turin Shroud as medieval? Or perhaps the real Shroud and its Grail are being worshipped in secret in some private chapel, or even mouldering, forgotten, in some castle.'

'Like this one?'

'I wish,' Jeremy said briefly.

Hazel was quiet for as long as it took to pour tea. 'The Grail would have been gold on silver?' she asked.

'There are those who say so, but I doubt it. Many of the early paintings show Christ emerging from a wooden box or casket – a strange concept unless this was the Grail. There's little or no doubt that it was of wood. Gilded and jewelled, I'd expect, but wood all the same.' He saw that Hazel looked disappointed. 'Did you think that you knew where it was?' he asked.

'It's my turn to wish,' she said.

All that day, she was thoughtful. By then, as they grew to understand each other's needs, their sex had come to deserve the description lovemaking. Each had been delighted to have found at last a partner devoted to giving as well as receiving pleasure. But during their passion that night she was noticeably distrait and Jeremy, for once, had to work hard.

Three

L ate winter was becoming early spring and for the next few days the weather held fair. Jeremy was gradually recovering his momentum in his work but Hazel was drawn to outdoors and turned her attention to the garden, tidying the few flowerbeds, readying the ancient lawnmower for the work soon to come and mounting a savage assault on the weeds which had invaded the gravel.

When several days had passed in this manner, she had identified several places which, she felt, were screaming to be filled with a mass of bulbs which neither she nor Jeremy could afford. An inconvenient break in the weather persuaded her back indoors to redeem her promise and carry out a hunt for disposable treasures. Perhaps a healthier balance in the bank might encourage Jeremy to spend some on bulbs and tubers. A conducted tour of the less used parts of the castle had produced nothing of any great interest which could be spared, much of the furnishings being in shabby condition and from bad periods. The few good pieces were of sentimental value or essential .to the habitability of the place.

Everything which looked potentially valuable had been removed to a cellar, Jeremy explained, and,

because he was so often away and the castle standing empty, that included everything which might be
attractive to the passing thief. He produced another
enormous key, remarking apologetically that he had
already picked over most of the bits and pieces in the
hope of treasure trove. What was left was damaged or,
to his inexpert eye, valueless. 'The dregs in the bottom
of the barrel,' he said.

'Would you recognize treasure if it spat in your eye?'
Hazel asked.

'Spit in my eye and I'll tell you.'

They descended a steep, stone stair into a large,
vaulted space, brightly lit by unshaded electric bulbs.
One of Jeremy's days for running the boiler and airing
the rooms above had just passed so that the cellar was
neither very cold nor more than slightly damp. Hazel
looked around in wonder.

'There are no bad vibes,' she said. 'Did your ancestors not do terrible things to their enemies down here?'

'My ancestors usually went in more for keeping their
heads down or being on the right side. Or sometimes
just retiring into the keep and daring the opposition to
come within range of an arrow or an arquebus. It seems
to have worked for them.'

'You wouldn't still happen to have that arquebus
around?'

'Sadly, no.'

Across the end wall, wine-racks were largely empty
but still held enough bottles to keep the pair of them
supplied for several years. Much of the remaining space
held damaged furniture on which had been randomly
deposited household items and objets d'art of china and
silver along with paintings and at least one tapestry.

31

'What's left is all chipped or broken or wormy,' Jeremy said. 'This is the junk-room.'

'You've got five hundred years of cast-offs in here. And it never occurred to you to get any repairs carried out?'

'More than five hundred. It occurred to me. But repairs cost money.'

'They may cost money but they can turn a wreck into an asset. Do you have any tools?'

It seemed an unlikely question. 'Tools?' Jeremy echoed vaguely.

'Tools. Chrissake!' she said impatiently. 'This is what I've been doing for years. I was never much good at buying or selling, and if I'd been in that sort of work I'd have had at least one decent dress to my name. But I'm a whizz at the three Rs. Repairs, renovations and restoration,' she explained when he looked baffled. She moved a broken lamp from a small table. 'Find me some good tools, emery paper, superglue and beeswax and I'll have the veneers refitted and the marquetry replaced and this table fit for the auction rooms within a week. Then I'd reckon to get twelve hundred for it, minimum. As it stands, eighty on a good day. And I won't charge you a dime provided only that you spend some of the money where I say, like on daffodil and tulip bulbs –' she toyed with the loose arm of a silver candelabrum – 'and some basic materials like silver solder.' She smiled suddenly, investing her face with added charm. 'And all I ask in return is bed and board and a good rogering now and again. And again.'

Jeremy gaped at her. 'That's the best offer I've had in the last thirty-three years,' he said at last.

'Is that how old you are?'

'Never mind how old I am. You'd better come with me.'

In what had once been a larder next to the boiler room, he showed her a toolbox holding a range of old but once good woodworking tools which she pronounced capable of being brought back to a useable state. Jeremy was dispatched in his car with a list of essential materials. He parted reluctantly from his work but accepted that, if Hazel was as good as her word, her efforts were more likely than his to produce a quick and sorely needed financial return.

For most of a day, Hazel busied herself sharpening chisels and planes and doctoring saws. The former larder – which, in keeping with the rest of the place, was huge in scale – became her workshop. After five more days, she carried the small table into the kitchen. The now perfect surfaces glowed richly. 'If you put cups down on this,' she said, 'I'll cut your pecker off. Remember, I have the tools to do it now.'

'That might be like cutting off your nose to spite your face,' he said mildly. 'It hasn't taken you long. And it looks good.'

'It *is* good. It came out of Edinburgh originally, so I guess that there or Glasgow is where to put it up for auction. There's a fancy bureau down below with all kinds of secret drawers and cubby-holes, Scottish, about seventeen-ninety. Should make about four thousand but it needs a lot of new working bits. You got any lumber I can cut up for bits?'

With a fresh stack of manuscript ready for copy-typing, Jeremy was not unwilling to turn his back on his work for a moment. He span his chair round. 'Not that I can think of,' he said. 'If you find any old furniture down there that isn't worth restoring, you could cut that up.'

'There's a big lump of timber against the far wall. Would anybody object if I cut it up?'

'There's nobody left to object except me. I see the sun's come out again. Let's go outside and enjoy it while I think.' Jeremy looked at the kitchen clock, a modern replica of a good carriage clock. 'The working day's about over. We'll take a beer with us. Bring a coat.'

Armed with lager, glasses and a pair of cushions, they took their now accustomed seats on the low wall. 'Still no midges,' she said.

'It's much too early for midges. If you're still here in the autumn, you'll know about it.' He paused. 'Will you still be here in the autumn?'

'By autumn, will you still want me here? No, don't answer that. It wasn't a fair question.' To bridge what she felt to be an awkward moment, she pointed out over the rolling moor, dotted with sheep. 'Does all that go with the castle?'

'Some of it. Around fifteen hundred acres.'

'There's a pattern of strips and stripes in the heather. Is that for the red grouse?'

'It was. We've given up, this last few years.' He gave a sigh. 'It's expensive, conserving for grouse – you have to keep burning in strips so that there's always heather of different ages; and you have to cut down on the sheep-grazing, for what little that brings in. We had to let the keeper go. You see, good grouse shooting can be very profitable – they come at you so damn fast that there's a cachet to being able to shoot them at all. But birds of prey are protected now, at the instigation of the Royal Society for the Protection of Birds at their dottiest. Hen harrier and peregrine nest numbers shot up at first, but when they'd killed most of their prey and, for us, conserving grouse stopped being viable, the numbers dropped back again. Now, with nobody culling foxes and weasels and carrion crows, the numbers of meadow pipits and skylarks are a fraction of what they used to be and lapwings and golden plover have almost disappeared. When the birds of prey have reduced their prey species still further, their numbers are going to settle down at a lower figure than they started at. Even the birdwatchers are beginning to demand that the RSPB change its tune.' He sighed again. 'If I wasn't so tied to this place, I'd move abroad to somewhere that the legislators have retained a vestige of common sense. Surely there's got to be somewhere.'

'I wouldn't bet on it,' Hazel said.

'No. Well, at least my occupation lets me go abroad now and again with a little help from the Inland Revenue.'

He obviously found the topic depressing. With a mental note to revive it on some other occasion, because any factor affecting Tinnisbeck Castle and its policies was beginning to fascinate her, she sought for another change of subject. 'What about that timber?' she asked.

'I don't know what to say. It has no value and yet there's a story attached to it.'

'Tell me,' she said. She had come particularly to enjoy the stories of his family.

'All right. It was the last voyage my parents made together before the one which ended their lives. They went round the Mediterranean and put in at Haifa. My father was worried because the mast step had a split in it. The boatbuilder he consulted didn't have a suitable balk of timber. Dad went ashore and found where they were pulling down an ancient temple to build a new mosque. He bought that slab of timber from the builder and hired a boy with a barrow to get it down to the boat. But by the time he got to the boatyard, the boatbuilder had already put a couple of bolts through the mast step and it was as solid as ever, and anyway Dad's timber turned out to be cedar, which would be too soft for the purpose. Dad brought it home as a souvenir and because no sailor with a wooden boat ever discards a good talk of timber. He left it in the cellar. It's been there ever since.'

'That's interesting,' Hazel said. 'But—'

'I haven't quite finished. Later, my grandfather heard about carbon-dating and, out of curiosity, he sent a sliver of the wood to a friend at Cambridge. The answer came back that the wood dated from the first or second century AD.'

Hazel choked on her lager and spluttered all over her jeans. Jeremy patted her on the back and lent her a handkerchief. 'You're supposed to swallow it,' he said. 'Not breathe it in. Or was it something I said?'

Hazel blew her nose, wiped her eyes and took several deep breaths. Dabbing ineffectually at her jeans she said, 'It was sure as hell something you said. Did you know that our very favouritest person, Gordon McKennerty, is hooked on the story of the Grail?'

'As a matter of fact, yes. That's how I came to know him well enough to let him rip me off over that figurine. The Historical Society hosted a conference about Lost Treasures in Edinburgh last summer. Vigo Bay and all that. I gave a talk about the Grail. Not that it's really my subject – as you know, I'm working on the Knights Templar – but of course the Shroud and the Grail keep popping up. Afterwards, Carmichael, the bookseller, introduced McKennerty to me. McKennerty wanted to debate one or two minor points with me, but in the main he agreed with what I'd been saying – pretty much what I was telling you. The subject seemed to fascinate him and he was more than averagely knowledgeable about it. Why do you have your knife so deep into him? Not just because you joined the ranks of the unemployed?'

'I'll tell you,' Hazel said. 'I was working for George Henderson – a sweet old guy but not the greatest businessman. On top of his other problems, he got his fingers burned with a set of Georgian chairs which turned out to have been stolen. And there was some stuff that never got paid for and a painting that turned out to be a fake. Just when he was getting desperate, the bank called his loan. He learned later that the bank had had a tip-off that he wasn't going to be able to meet his liabilities. Then Gordon McKennerty came up with an offer for the shop which would just about clear his debts. While George was hesitating, somebody went for him in the street, after dark. He took the hint and sold out.'

'You think that McKennerty was behind it?'

'What do you think? We knew that McKennerty must have spotted something but we couldn't figure what. Turned out to be one of a stack of grotty old canvasses. It was covered with dark varnish and splashed with emulsion paint, but when it was cleaned up it was a moonlight scene, oils on wood, by Van Schendel, and it went for ninety grand in auction at Christie's.'

'Rotten but perfectly legal,' Jeremy commented.

'My turn to be not quite finished. McKennerty bought the shop for a song on the understanding that he would settle all debts. I was due more than six months' salary and I never saw a dime of it. When I complained, McKennerty suggested that I sue him, and hinted that I might get the dark alley treatment before it came near court. I believed him. The word is that several people who really got across him haven't been seen walking around any more. That's how come I was so broke when we met up. George Henderson died around that time, overdosed on whisky and aspirin. Now do you see why McKennerty isn't my favourite person?'

Jeremy nodded sadly. 'I wish I'd known all that before he approached me. I hadn't met him before but I'd heard of his interest in antiques, so I asked him if he could recommend a dealer who I could trust.' He laughed bitterly. 'That was about like Red Riding Hood asking the wolf to recommend a good babysitter. You know the story?' he asked.

'I know the story,' she said. 'We're not entirely cut off from civilization in the States.'

'We'll discuss that another time. So what's McKennerty got to do with you trying to breathe in half a pint of lager?'

She half-turned on the wall to look at him full-face. 'Just this. We both owe McKennerty a grudge and a half and you could argue that he owes us each a ton of money. McKennerty's interest in the Grail's well known in the antiques trade, so when you were telling me about the Grail I was thinking that a casket of silver criss-crossed with strips of gold would be kind of easy to fake. Expensive, maybe, but not too difficult. You'd have to get the alloys just right, but otherwise metals don't give much away. Oxidize the silver and you're about there. But then you went and said that the Grail was timber. So I tried to put it out of my mind but I guess it was still burrowing away in there. And now you tell me that you have a slab of timber of the right age sitting right here in your basement and a letter to tell you the age of it. You do have the letter?' she asked anxiously.

'Somewhere.'

'There you are, then. Between us we have the knowledge, the skill and most of the materials. What say we make up a Grail, just like you said it would be? It needn't even cost much – a few hundred at the most. If McKennerty thought he was getting away with the real thing under our noses, how much do you think he'd pay for it?'

Jeremy got to his feet and walked in a circle on the dry grass. Hazel watched him fondly and waited. The idea would take some swallowing.

He came back and stood over her. 'But could we do it?'

'I could do most of it,' she said. 'It wouldn't be far off what I've been doing for years. We'd have to fake up some extra provenance.'

'The timber's only cedar.'

'Just what they'd use to make a box to keep a linen cloth in. Proof against insects,' Hazel explained.

'But the cost! It would have been gilded and encrusted with precious stones.'

'Gilding is easy. Gold leaf goes a long way. Any

precious or semi-precious stones would surely have been dug out of it and sold years ago. Centuries ago. That wouldn't diminish the basic value of an incredible relic. Easy enough to fake where they'd been. Think about it. Almost everything we need has fallen into our laps. It's as if it was meant.'

'No,' he said. 'No. It's impossible. Not to be thought of.'

But she could hear the uncertainty in his voice and she left the idea to simmer. 'OK,' she said. 'You've a nice pair of quaichs down below. Tomorrow, I'll set about pressing out a few dents and cleaning them up a bit. When I've finished with them, you'll be amazed what they'll fetch.'

'I don't usually like surprises but I'll tolerate that one,' he said.

'While I go and get on with dinner, you drive down to the service station and bring me back a glass-fibre car-repair kit.'

By then, Jeremy knew that there was always a good reason for her more bizarre requests. He fished in his pocket for the car keys.

With the repair kit, Hazel made a male and a female mould from an undamaged section of one of the quaichs and set about squeezing dents out of the pair and teasing the metal back into shape. As she told Jeremy, 'If you beat metal back into place you stretch it. Then it never goes back quite right.'

After three days, he found her sitting out on a cushion on the wall with the quaichs, some cloths and a tin of silver polish, taking the sun and smoothing away the last residual roughness. 'That's amazing,' he said. 'I could have sworn that those were beyond repair.'

Hazel rotated one of the quaichs, admiring her own reflection and inspecting for flaws. 'It takes genius,' she admitted.

'I can't argue with that. Where would be the best place to sell these and the table? It's time we had some money in the bank. We're going to need it.'

She took note of his last sentence but let it go by without comment. 'I know a collector in Glasgow who might buy the quaichs,' she said, 'and there's a good auction house there I could talk to about the table.'

'Suits me. I want to see Carmichael about some books. If the weather holds, we could go tomorrow. Are you ready?'

'I'll be ready by then.'

'Great! But we'll need a dry day, because my car won't carry the table unless I take the top down.'

She put the quaich down very carefully. 'There's just one thing,' she said. 'I don't have clothes for talking to collectors and auctioneers. You have to look kosher or they wave you away. They think you stole whatever it is. You'll have to do the talking. I can tell you what to say.'

Jeremy's beard twitched uncertainly. 'I still couldn't carry it off. If they asked me a question you hadn't already briefed me on, I'd be sunk and they'd be sure I was a fence. If we get the sort of money you're talking about, I'll buy you a whole new wardrobe. Stand up a moment.' She stood and he surveyed her critically. 'When my mother was killed, my grandfather gave away most of her clothes to charity, but some of them were too good for that. I think they're still in the wardrobe. And you don't have to look at me as if I was trying to get you into a crinoline. A good tartan skirt never dates. Or not very much.'

Four

The morning came in dry and clear. Jeremy looked out as he dressed. 'The forecast's good,' he said. 'Anyone who believes weather forecasts will believe a politician's promise, but this time they could be right.'

Hazel felt strange and out of place in a tweed skirt, cashmere twinset, silk headsquare and brogues, all once the property of Jeremy's mother and a passable fit for herself. She was sure that she was an outlandish figure but Jeremy assured her that she looked the very image of a modish lady visiting town from the Scottish countryside and, although she had reservations as to the value of his opinion when it came to matters of feminine couture, she was reassured. Her image was spoiled for the moment when they realized that she lacked any coat warm enough for travelling in an open car in early spring. Jeremy lent her a duffel-coat to wear over her anorak.

The soft-top of Jeremy's car was lowered and the small table, wrapped in old blankets, was lodged upright behind the seats. A parcel of books was put into the boot and the quaichs, well padded, were wedged in beside it. The seats had to be moved forward to allow the table into a space which had never been intended to hold more than the occasional child, but they could manage. Jeremy drove with his knees and elbows uncomfortably bent.

Between wind-noise and the music of the exhaust, conversation was inhibited during the twenty minutes of country roads and nearly an hour of dual carriageway. They crested the final hill at last and saw the conurbation spread across the Clyde before them. As they slowed for the Glasgow speed restrictions he said, 'Auction house first, I think. Direct me.'

'If we sold the quaichs first, I could get more suitable clothes.'

'You couldn't get anything more suitable. And I want to get this table out of the car before I slip a disc or the rain comes on.'

Reluctantly, she admitted that he had a point. She resigned herself to appearing in public as a figure of fun. 'If you say so. Head for the city centre and I'll tell you where to turn off.'

Traffic was moving slowly so that conversation was easy. 'I found the letter about the carbon-dating,' he said.

'I'd like to see it when we get back. It might be difficult to let him have a sight of it without being too obvious and making him think too much.'

The auctioneers had offices in a modern building near City Square. They parked in the multi-storey car park. Jeremy lifted out the table and erected the top while Hazel shed the ungainly outer garments and restored order to her hair with his comb. 'This doesn't feel like me any more,' she said, 'but I suppose the real me is still inside here somewhere. You still want to leave this to me?'

'I'm determined to.' Jeremy had no confidence in his own ability to conduct negotiations over antiques. He shouldered the table. 'Do they know your face?' he asked.

'I doubt it. Not to recognize, out of context, in fuddy-duddy clothes and with my hair different.'

'So you're the lady of the castle,' he said. 'I'd better pass for your ghillie or manservant. Call yourself Mrs Carpenter and arrange for the cheque to be made out to Mr J. Carpenter.'

'I don't have a wedding ring.'

'Miss Carpenter, then. You can be the laird's sister.'

The chill brought her out in goose-pimples but there was no suitable shop in sight. Hazel hurried to the auction rooms. She knew who to ask for and a businesslike gentleman with a brown coat over a good business suit came out to meet them.

'I'll get back to the car, miss,' Jeremy said. Without quite tugging his forelock, he escaped back to the car park. The boot was still securely locked. The radio refused to play within the confines of the car-park building. He paced between the rows of cars.

Hazel rejoined him in fifteen minutes, warming her hands under her armpits. 'Back over the Clyde,' she said. 'The man we want lives in Govanhill, near Queen's Park.' They ducked into the car and adjusted the seats. When they were out in the street, the radio suddenly came alive. Hazel switched it off. She turned the heater up to maximum and held her fingers over the vent. 'The table goes into a sale they're holding at Gleneagles at the end of next month. We were just in time to get it included in the catalogue. Overseas buyers will be bidding over the phone. I set a reserve price of twelve hundred but I'll be sick if we don't do a lot better.'

Jeremy raised his eyebrows. He made no further comment but mused cheerfully on the prospect of being able to run the castle's central heating for the rest of the year.

They stopped in one of the tree-lined streets of large Victorian houses which surprise the stranger in Glasgow. 'Leave it to me again?'

'With pleasure. You know the man and you know the small-talk.'

'But will he know me, dressed up like your Queen Mum's great-aunt? I'll try to get a deposit,' Hazel said. 'But we won't get cash on the barrel-head. This guy's cautious. He'll want to check that they aren't on the stolen list.'

'Sensible chap.'

Jeremy listened to the radio. It was almost a hour before Hazel came back, minus the bundle. 'I'm better at selling than I knew,' she said. 'You should have seen his little face light up. I got two hundred cash, which was all that he and his wife had in the house between them, and a post-dated cheque. How does this grab you?'

He scanned the cheque and his eyes opened wide. It was dated a week ahead. 'I don't know how it grabs me,' he said huskily, 'but it grabs me. You really are something. Some of this is yours.'

'I'm holding on to the two hundred for expenses unless you need it.' She handed over an envelope. 'You'd better keep the letter of agreement. This is just in case he changes his mind. Where to now?'

'Edinburgh. I want to visit Carmichael.'

'OK. From here on, I'm just along for the ride. But you love your books, don't you?' she asked anxiously. 'You don't have to sell any more of them, with that cheque in your pocket.'

He laughed and started the car. 'Bless you for the kind thought. But I'm always buying books. If I kept them all, the castle would soon run out of shelf-space. Carmichael buys them back from me for almost what I paid. In the meantime I've used the computer and the scanner to copy onto disks any of the passages I want to refer to again.'

'Is that legal?'

'I think so. It's for my personal use. No worse than photocopying.'

They turned off the motorway to find lunch at a former mansion, now a top-of-the-range hotel and gourmet restaurant. With notes in his wallet and the prospect of money to come from the table, Jeremy insisted that they ate well, but they were soon back on the road. After coming within an inch of disaster on one of Edinburgh's huge roundabouts, where the lane priorities change suddenly and are only demarked by a shift of the road numbers on the road surface, to the inevitable confusion of visitors, they plunged into Edinburgh's older streets.

Hazel turned her face away as they passed the former shop, now a wine-bar. From her local knowledge, she was able to direct him to a little-known parking place. Jeremy retrieved his heavy parcel from the boot. 'You don't have to come in,' he said. 'You could be warm in the wine-bar.'

She looked at him suspiciously. 'You're kidding! That's the last place I'd want to hang around. Too many memories. I'm coming with you.' Resolutely, she donned the duffel-coat again. With the dealing over, appearances had become secondary.

Carmichael's had a narrow street frontage but it went deep into the block, spreading as it went. The atmosphere was hushed, the air dusty. The floor had sunk into strange inclines under the great weight of knowledge. Half a dozen or more assistants were needed to keep the stock in order, so it was some time before Mr Carmichael himself realized that an old and valued customer was prowling the shelves. Mr Carmichael was a tubby, bustling little man in his fifties, with high colour, little hair and a permanent expression of pleased surprise.

He found Jeremy, as usual, in the European Medieval History section and waited patiently until the shelves had been picked over.

'You've found what you want?'

'All that I can afford,' Jeremy said. 'I left a parcel of books at the desk. And I'd like a word.'

'Of course.'

Hazel met them at the desk and showed Jeremy a stout and dusty copy of *A History of Cabinet-Making*, bound in the style of the early twentieth century. Without a word, she handed it to Jeremy. He nodded and she left the shop.

In Mr Carmichael's office, a cash adjustment was agreed.

'Now, Mr Carpenter, what else can I do for you?'

Jeremy had been wondering how to arrive at his subject but he decided that a plunge was the best approach. 'Do you remember introducing Gordon McKennerty to me in the Conference Centre?'

Mr Carmichael looked flustered. 'I had no alternative,' he said. 'He's a very . . . regular customer and he was most insistent. I thought that you probably knew his reputation. I do hope . . .'

'You weren't to blame,' Jeremy said, 'but I didn't know as much of his reputation as I do now and it cost me. So now – and this is in the very strictest confidence – I'm looking for a chance to recoup my losses. I take it that Mr McKennerty is not a friend as well as a regular customer?'

'Certainly not,' said the bookseller. His round and rosy face flushed darkly so that what remained of his silver hair looked brighter. He lowered his voice and sounded flustered. 'Do be careful. Between you and me, Mr Carpenter, Gordon McKennerty is a bad lot. He entertains constantly and some of his house guests you wouldn't want to meet after dark. He seems so friendly, but if you cross him his face goes cold and his voice drops and he never quite says anything aloud but there are hints, half-concealed threats. And he means them. Somehow I've let him run up a very large account and when I threatened legal action . . . well, it may have been coincidence, but the very next day a pair of toughs visited my home, roughed up my wife and helped themselves to some of my property. The police were told, but there was little or no evidence and they were impotent. And now, of course, I daren't even refuse him when he asks for some expensive item to be charged to his account. I don't want to end up in the Forth, weighted down,' Carmichael finished bitterly.

Jeremy sighed. 'I'm sorry. It seems that we're in much the same boat. I won't ask you to put yourself at risk, but I could use some information.'

'Anything, Mr Carpenter. Anything at all.'

'Do you have a description of the two toughs who visited Mrs Carmichael?'

'Fragmentary, I'm afraid. I never saw them and my wife was too upset to remember any details. They said very little but she had the impression that they were both Scots but comparatively well spoken. One was larger than the other, for what that's worth – she couldn't say how large.'

'Let me know if she remembers any more,' Jeremy said. 'I'd prefer to recognize them if they turn up on my doorstep some day. Is he still interested in the Shroud and the Grail?'

'Very much so.' The bookseller seemed relieved to get back to a subject that was more nearly business. 'I have a standing instruction to let him know of anything new that comes in, touching on the subjects. That's in addition to his getting my catalogue of new acquisitions every quarter. And now he's showing a special interest in fourteenth-century Germany.'

'Is he?' Jeremy said. 'Is he indeed? You might care to draw his attention to the last few pages of the J. C. Lester book I've just returned to you. Let me know if he makes any other special requests. Or if anything special turns up in either field.'

'Of course, Mr Carpenter.'

Hazel was not at the car nor in the wine-bar. She turned up at the car after twenty minutes, carrying packages. Jeremy made no comment. She would tell him when the time was ripe. He concentrated on making it safely through the Edinburgh traffic with the low sun shining in his eyes. 'Who are these toughs that

McKennerty seems able to whistle up when he wants them?' he asked.

'If you've got money, you can get toughs. From what I've heard, he cultivates the wilder element among the rugger-buggers, as I've heard them called. The way I think it is, most men go in for Rugby because it's a sport that's great for a tough man to play; but others start off as tough men and they go in for Rugby because it's an outlet for their toughness. Some of those wouldn't think twice about breaking an arm or a leg to please a pal or a generous host. You see the difference?'

'I see it all right.'

Jeremy was silent for the next twenty miles. 'Mc-Kennerty seems to be taking an interest in fourteenth-century Germany,' he said suddenly. 'That suggests that he's trying to trace the Grail's travels after it left France. Assuming that we get the funds which seem to be coming our way from this trip, would you know where we could pick up some paper that could pass for fourteenth-century German?'

Hazel kept her voice bland. 'I think I could manage that,' she said.

'Expensive?'

'A hundred or so.'

Jeremy mused in silence. Hazel left him to his thoughts. He would admit her to them when he was good and ready. Time and more miles went by.

The ruin of her car was still at the roadside. The bonnet was up and it now lacked wheels. She looked the other way. The car did not owe her anything. She had had her money's worth and more out of it.

They were almost back at Tinnisbeck Castle when

Jeremy spoke so suddenly that she jumped. 'I can imagine a very guarded letter from de Charnay's connection, Otto von Henneberg, to one of my ancestors. I could manage the medieval Latin, with the aid of a dictionary. I can do a passable Gothic script. I don't suppose any of von Henneberg's handwriting still exists – if he could write, which I'd better check. But I wouldn't know about ink.'

'I can find out about ink,' Hazel said. 'And I could see to the ageing of the document. I've got most of what I'd need in those carrier bags. I went to a chemist and an art supplier for what I'll need to age my repairs to some of your other goodies.'

'You,' Jeremy said with laughter in his voice, 'are not a very reputable character.'

Hazel pretended indignation. 'Repairs and renovations are quite legal. In fact, if an item has any genuinely antique components in it at all, it's quite legal to sell it as an antique.'

'I'll be damned. You mean, you could take a table apart and make five tables, each with one genuine leg or a top, and call each of them a genuine antique?'

'It happens all the time,' Hazel said.

They never acknowledged aloud their intention to go ahead, but that evening, in Jeremy's presence, Hazel phoned a number in outer London.

'Charlie?' she said. 'Charlie Adams? Hazel Tripp. I came down to see you about the illuminated letter some horse's ass had cut out of the Da Crema manuscript. Remember? You do? Charlie, could you put your hands on a sheet of paper that could pass for fourteenth-century German? That'd be great. And, Charlie, how about ink to match? Tell me the ingredients and I can mix it for myself . . . OK, send me a bottle.' She picked up a sheet of notepaper bearing Jeremy's neat script. 'Send it to me, care of Ian Argyll, Bruisbeck Cottage, Cauldshielknowe . . .' She spelled out the name and quoted the postcode. 'And this is confidential. A hundred and twenty, all up?' Jeremy nodded. 'Right. The cheque will be in the post tomorrow.' She broke the connection. 'Confidential always costs a little more. Who is this guy Ian Argyll?'

'He started life as my grandfather's general handyman. Now he has the local joinery business. He also owns the pub. He's related to almost everybody around these parts and he cuts a lot of ice, but you wouldn't know it. I think he still thinks of himself as a member of the castle entourage. It's time you met him. You may want his help in cutting up that timber. Or must it be kept away from machine tools?'

'A bandsaw would be a hell of a help,' Hazel said. 'If I use hand tools from there on, no way could anybody tell the difference. I hope he's good. We only get one shot at this, unless you have another source of two-thousand-year-old timber. You'll have to give me a clue to the design.'

'He's good. I'll give you all I've got in the morning. No drawings exist but we can infer almost everything from other examples and from what's been written. Who's this Charlie and how does he come to have paper that nobody else has got?'

'He's a specialist. He does some work himself, and brilliantly, much of it quite legit, but mostly he's a dealer in rare papers. He buys up books which are beyond salving, old missals that Victorian ladies have cut the illuminated letters out of for their scrapbooks and all like that, so's he can get the fly-leaves and endpapers. Old Bibles often had a whole lot of blank pages for writing in the family history.'

'And he won't talk?'

'He couldn't stay in business if he was a loud-mouth.'

'I suppose that's true.'

Hazel settled to a study of the history of cabinet-making.

In the morning, after the cheque had been posted to Charlie, Jeremy hunted first through his index and then through a small group of floppy disks until he found an illustration of one of the Nuremburg boxes. 'The folded Shroud is said to be just under four feet by two,' he said, 'and less than three inches thick. Translated into metric—'

'Don't bother,' Hazel said. 'I'm only a damn Yankee, remember, and I don't suppose your Ian Argyll has converted to metric yet. What else have you got?'

Jeremy hunted out and printed every reference which he had ever found bearing on the design to be expected of the Grail, and all the medieval artwork from which inferences had been drawn. After covering several A4 pages with sketches and calculations, Hazel arrived at a cutting pattern which would produce the optimum reduction of the balk of cedar into useable timber.

Jeremy, who had reluctantly returned to acting as his own typist, spent the day at his computer while Hazel reglued the veneers on a Victorian marquetry sewing-box, but each was too preoccupied to make much progress. Both were relieved when Jeremy announced that the pub in the village would be open.

The boot of the car would not close on the balk of

cedar. Jeremy drove very carefully down the uneven drive for fear of damaging the car. The village was a cluster of stone buildings, a church, a small green and a bridge. In the only bar, a newly lit fire was crackling in the grate.

A sturdy man of around fifty, in dusty overalls and a cloth cap, came through from the back and took his place behind the bar. 'Evening, Mr Carpenter.' His voice was warm.

'Good evening, Ian. This is Hazel. We'll have drams and have one yourself.' Hazel was amused to notice that Jeremy's voice was now softened by an unaffected trace of the local accent.

The customary few minutes had to be spent in discussion of the weather and exchanging fragments of local news, before Jeremy said, 'We have a balk of timber in the car to be sawn, Ian. Can you help us out?'

'H'm. Any nails in't?'

Jeremy looked at Hazel, who said, 'None at all.'

'Nae bother, then. Come awa through.' He called to some anonymous voice in the back premises to keep an eye on the bar.

'Perhaps we should have caught you during the day?' Hazel suggested. She added a little water to her whisky, aware of the critical eyes of the men watching to see whether she drowned it.

'Ye couldna. I've been awa at Dunnet's Farm, fitting windows.'

They carried their drinks out through the back of the pub, past the hairdresser's small establishment and into a barnlike building behind the kirk. While Jeremy went back to the car for the timber, Hazel satisfied herself that the machines were well kept, the saw blades sharp and precise. Among the good modern tools on the shelves were some older tools, even some valuable antiques among them.

'You'll be a friend of Mr Carpenter?' Ian Argyll asked suddenly.

'Yes.'

'You're staying at the castle?'

This was none of his damn business, but they needed his help. Also, the enquiries seemed to be made out of friendly interest rather than curiosity and Hazel was sure that Jeremy would be offended if she quarrelled with his friend. She said yes again.

'It's been a long while since there was a woman at the castle. You'll be biding a whilie?'

'We haven't decided yet,' Hazel said loftily.

Ian considered her quietly for a few seconds. 'Likely you will,' he said.

The return of Jeremy with the balk over his shoulder cut short that topic. The joiner moved quickly. 'Hey! Let me gie you a hand wi that.'

'It's cedar,' Jeremy said. 'Not as heavy as it looks. But you can help me down with it.'

With the timber on the bench, Hazel produced her diagram and after an earnest consultation the first cutting lines were marked. Ian adjusted his fences and began to cut. While conversation was impossible, Hazel kept away from the flying sawdust and instead studied the old tools and took a cautious sniff at several old glue-pots.

After the first few cuts it was clear that the timber contained no serious flaws. It could have been rotten at heart, although cedar, she knew, is not usually attractive to fungi and borers. When the cutting was finished and Ian had been dissuaded from passing the boards over the machine planer, she let Jeremy carry the load back to the car while she had a word with the joiner.

Jeremy returned, brushing dust from his jacket. 'Ian,' he said, 'for the moment, Hazel is Miss Carpenter. My sister. And not for the reason you're thinking of,' he added firmly. 'I'll explain some day. For the moment, just accept that it's important. If any stranger should come poking around, asking questions, that's what to tell them. Will you spread the word?'

'I'll do that,' Ian said simply.

She rejoined Jeremy carrying a laden plastic carrier bag.

'What were you and Ian confabulating about?' he asked as he drove.

'He wanted to know if we're an item and I gave him an evasive answer – a surprisingly polite one in the circumstances. In return, I borrowed an old grooving plane and some glue. I wanted a traditional glue which wouldn't betray its age so I took a glue-pot left over from his grandfather's day. It'll probably stink the place out when I put it on to melt.'

'Oh well. This old castle's had some funny smells in its day. I don't suppose another one will matter.'

For several days a sort of peace reigned, except for the delivery of a mountain of coke. Jeremy pretended to be writing but spent most of each day deep in thought. Hazel had vanished into her makeshift workshop, emerging occasionally to ask questions . . .

When Jeremy walked down to the village to beg a

pair of thin plastic gloves from the hairdresser – 'What are those for?'

'I shan't want my fingerprints on the letter,' he explained.

'Oh. Will it matter if my prints are all over the box?'

'Not in the least. Some day, we may want to prove that it isn't the real thing.'

Hazel thought for a minute. 'Got you,' she said. 'That's clever.'

On another occasion – 'What about hinges?'

'If it ever had hinges, they would have been added later. Leave them out. Make it a nice rebated, lift-off lid.'

And again – 'What about the glass panel in the lid?'

'That was added later. Make it without for the moment.'

'Are you going to get the right glass?'

'Almost impossible. Anyway, the glass would certainly have been broken during a couple of millennia of being smuggled around, bumped about and saved from a fire. I suppose, on those grounds, we could get away with a later glass, but nothing modern. Safer to have it broken and missing.'

'Fire?'

'Yes. The Turin Shroud has a pattern of scorch-marks corresponding to the folded state.'

And later – 'Would the inside be gilded?'

Jeremy had to think about that one. 'Just plain wood,' he said at last.

'So it would be well oxidized by now.'

'A few days in the sunshine should take care of

that. But it's supposed to be stained with Christ's sweat and blood. It would have to be human blood – that's one thing that's too easily tested. I suppose,' Jeremy said, 'that either of us could bleed into it. They won't have any of His DNA to compare it with.'

'You can bleed into it,' Hazel said. 'I'll supply a little sweat – I'm producing plenty of that – and I'll age the blood for you.'

After three days, things happened. Shortly after breakfast, Jeremy, who had been excluded from the workshop, was invited to see the work as far as it had progressed.

He penetrated into the small workshop where the air was tainted with the smell of glue, melting over a small electric ring. The large flat box was embellished with a diamond pattern in thin strips of cedar. The wood glowed palely under the artificial light. The lid was a perfect fit.

'That's very good,' he said. 'More than very good. It's brilliant. I'm impressed out of my mind. Those dovetails are perfection.'

'Thank you. Maybe I overdid it. They can't be seen from inside, and the outside will be gold-leafed.'

'I'm sorry to break it to you,' he said lightly, 'but this beautiful creation is going to have a rough time. All kinds of things would have been dropped on it over the centuries and, remember, the Shroud shows signs of a fire. That may have happened before or after the two were separated, we don't know for sure, but it would add a touch of verification if we scorch a couple of corners after it's complete. Your beautiful dovetails may well see the light of day again.'

Hazel sighed and stroked the box. 'My lovely Grail, was it for this that I created you? But it's in a good cause. Next thing, I want gold leaf. I gild the outside before I make the viewing window?'

'Definitely yes. Where do we get gold leaf?'

'I can get it through the post. Or I know a place in Edinburgh.'

'Do it by phone and post. We don't want to make any ripples in Edinburgh. Meanwhile, a few days in the sunshine wouldn't come amiss. For the Grail, I mean, not ourselves.'

As Jeremy pointed out, they could hardly put the box and lid out on the terrace where any casual visitor would see them and become curious. Instead, they climbed the peel and placed them where they would catch the sun which, that day, was showing promise of spring and summer to come. Hazel would have lingered to admire the view from the roof, but a van was approaching, bouncing carelessly over the potholes.

They reached the main doorway as Ian Argyll descended from the van. He handed Jeremy a large envelope and a small packet. 'These came for you. Morning, Miss Carpenter.'

'Good morning,' Jeremy said on behalf of them both. 'You'll take a dram, Ian?'

The invitation seemed to be expected. Ian followed them into the kitchen, but there he seemed to suffer a change of mind. 'Better no,' he said. 'The bobby's on the prowl wi his wee breathalyser. How are you daein' wi yon timmer?' he asked Hazel.

'I haven't made a start yet,' she said. The joiner looked down at her jeans, powdered with fine sawdust. 'Except to sand off the first piece,' she resumed quickly. 'I'm going to make Jeremy a fitment to take his computer disks and reference books.'

The joiner hesitated. Hazel decided that he was one of the brigade of experts who enjoy foisting their help on the amateur whether wanted or not. 'I could ha gien ye a wheen of timmer for that,' he said.

Jeremy put a hand on the older man's shoulder and gently led him outside. 'There was no need, when we had that block sitting around and begging to be used. We'll invite you up to christen it with a dram and criticism when it's finished.'

As the van bumped away down the drive, Hazel said, 'Now I'll have to make you that fitment.'

'That's right.'

'Rank opportunism!' Hazel said, laughing.

She telephoned to an art suppliers in Chelsea and was promised the immediate dispatch of a dozen sheets of gold leaf. As soon as she disconnected, the phone rang again. A voice which she seemed to have heard before asked for Jeremy.

He took he phone. 'Mr Carpenter?' said the voice. 'This is Andrew Carmichael. It might be to your advantage to come and see me.'

'What about?'

There was a pause. 'It's not a matter for discussing on the phone, as I think you'll agree if we meet. I don't know who could be overhearing your end and you don't know about mine. I can't leave the shop. Will you pay me a visit? I've found that copy of Hubert Graves you asked me about.'

'When would suit you?'

'The sooner the better.'

'I'll come straight away.'

'The very attractive young lady who was with you . . . If she's in your confidence, it might be an advantage if you brought her along.'

Jeremy gave Hazel the gist of the message. 'Carmichael described you as very attractive,' he added.

'He had me confused with somebody else,' Hazel said.

'I'd have recognized the description anywhere,' Jeremy told her.

Five

A fter several anxious glances at the sky and a quick reference to Teletext, they decided that it was not going to rain and that the Grail could safely be left on the roof to darken in the UV rays of a sun which shone brightly above a chill breeze. Hazel changed into what she called her going-to-town clothes. Rather than sully them with the despised duffel-coat, she insisted that Jeremy warm the car's engine before she entered it and then dropped the coat behind the seats.

'We'll have to buy you a warm coat,' Jeremy said. 'I owe you that much and more.'

Hazel threw him a warm glance. 'Don't worry about it,' she said. 'I'm not a sociable sort of person and I don't give a damn for possessions. I never hang on to money for long.'

'You do give a damn about being cold. I need you to play the part of the mistress of a castle. If you look like a pauper wearing her brother's cast-offs, McKennerty will decide that a few hundred would be beyond your dreams of avarice. Where does your money go?'

'I couldn't tell you. I guess it sort of melts.'

'How did you survive an Edinburgh winter with only that anorak thing to pull on?'

'I lived near my work and had an umbrella.'

'God! And they say that we Scots are hardy!'

One door and the rear seat had vanished from Hazel's car. As they went by, he saw that the rear sub-frame had also disappeared. 'Somebody's building a trailer,' he said.

'And the best of luck to him.'

They were silent for a few miles. Jeremy stole a quick glance at her profile. She was obviously deep in thought. A little later, she said, 'I don't know what Mr Carmichael wants, but this may be the last moment for turning back. I've no doubts about the ethics of what we're trying on. We're the goodies on white horses and McKennerty's the baddy in a black hat. But are we being blasphemous?'

The question took Jeremy by surprise. 'I don't think so,' he said. 'Can you really believe, with your mind, in a personal God?'

In his peripheral vision, he saw her hands lift and then fall in a gesture of helplessness. 'That's a question and a half and not even the same question as mine. I was brought up a Catholic and to believe that every word in the Bible is truth, but as I grew up I found that blind faith was too much to ask. I looked around and saw things I could believe in and understand and nothing at all that seemed to come from anything paranormal. Common sense suggested that Darwin had the right of it. So I'm torn between my heart, which still wants to go along with my upbringing, and my brain, which suggests I go down on my knees and worship the Big Bang. I guess I'm agnostic. And proud of it – I think.'

'That's quite witty,' Jeremy said. 'You don't usually make conscious jokes.'

'It happens sometimes. What about you?'

After a few seconds of thought, Jeremy put the question into its context. He spoke absently, most of his mind to threading through the traffic. 'I can't believe in a personal God. Like you, I find that the concept stretches credulity just a little too far. If I'm wrong, I'll apologize when I meet Him. I believe that Christ was a real person, but evidence coming out of the Dead Sea Scrolls suggests that the spiritual legends about him stem from St Paul, who had a stroke on the road to Damascus and suffered hallucinations which he believed to be visions. I accept that Christ was crucified, but for political reasons, and that's about as far as I can go. Carbon-dating indicated that the Turin Shroud is a medieval fake or substitute, perhaps to replace an original which burned. But, by the way, carbon-dating can be wrong. There was a case a few years ago. A man was suspected of having buried his wife's body in boggy ground near his house. Contractors laying a pipeline turned up a human, female skull. The man confessed to the murder of his wife. Then carbon-dating put the skull at hundreds of years old, which made it the irony of the century. But later still, it turned out that it could have been her skull after all.'

'The chemistry of the boggy ground?'

'Exactly. So it's quite possible that the Shroud is genuine. That the Grail legend refers to the casket which had once contained the Shroud seems highly probable. But I don't intend to promise anybody that ours is the true Grail. If some greedy person assumes that it's so, that's their false assumption, stemming from the same sort of wishful thinking that lies behind most religious beliefs. So, given the many breaks in the chain linking it with a genuinely divine being, I'd say no. Not blasphemous.'

Hazel sighed. Jeremy interpreted the sigh as being of relief. 'OK,' she said. 'Part of me's glad, part doesn't give a damn and another part's sorry if there's nothing beyond this life. Well, whatever. Go get 'em, cowboy!'

They crossed the ring road and plunged into the traffic of Edinburgh, arriving safely at last in the vicinity of the Royal Mile. They left the car in the same secluded car park as before. The day was cool but Hazel, who was beginning, rather late in life, to take a pride in her appearance, insisted that she could walk as far as Carmichael's shop without spoiling her image by wearing the duffel-coat. The tourist season was beginning and they had to elbow their way between wanderers and shoppers.

In the shop, they met a snag. Mr Carmichael was out. Jeremy suspected that this was an evasive tactic. 'He's expecting us,' he told the girl at the cash-desk.

The girl was young, straggle-haired and anxious to please. 'I know that, Mr Carpenter. There's somebody he wants you to meet. He said to tell you that he'll meet you in the wine-bar between two and two-thirty.'

'So be it,' Jeremy said.

If they went back for the car, they might never get parked again. Hazel was beginning to shiver. Without a word, Jeremy steered her into a shop and made her try on coats. She drew the line at the expensive sheepskin but was persuaded at last to accept a smart tweed which more or less harmonized with the skirt. Jeremy paid with a credit card.

'I didn't know that you could afford that kind of extravagance,' Hazel said as they turned into the Royal Mile.

'I can easily afford it. Just so long as that cheque clears before my credit card account is due for settlement. You're bringing in much more than that.'

'Well, OK. But it was your own goodies that I fixed up. I don't like owing anybody.'

'Idiot!' Jeremy said fondly. 'But for you, the goodies, as you call them, would have stayed in the cellar until they mouldered, got sold for peanuts or chopped up for firewood. You don't owe me a damn thing.'

Hazel stroked the lapel of her new coat. 'I owe you more than you know,' she said quietly. 'But thank you, anyway.'

They found a small café which was serving lunches and not too crowded. They lingered over the meal. When it was finished, they were back in the street. They arrived at the doorway of the wine-bar shortly before two-thirty. Hazel hung back. 'I don't know that I want to go back in there,' she said. 'I spent too many happy years there and then had to watch it being . . . raped.'

'Face your fears.' Jeremy led her firmly inside. 'In ten minutes, it will be just another wine-bar.'

Hazel braced herself and then led the way firmly, deep into the long room. The lunchtime crowd was thinning out and they found a vacant table. 'This is exactly where my bench was,' Hazel said sadly. 'I could kill that guy McKennerty, I really could. It was a great little business here and I enjoyed it, restoring all those beautiful old treasures.'

'It didn't bother you that they weren't your own treasures?'

67

'No way! Let somebody else worry about fires and burglars and insurance and the help being careless. It was enough for me that they existed. That made me feel good.' The waitress arrived to take their order. 'If you want a drink,' Hazel said, 'I can drive.'

'I'll take it easy,' Jeremy said. He ordered a spritzer. Hazel asked for a glass of the house red.

'Are you Mr Carpenter?' the waitress asked. 'Because we close for the afternoon and open again at five, but Mr Carmichael arranged with the boss that you can stay on for your talk. They play golf together,' she added, as though that explained everything.

'Don't you trust me?' Hazel asked as the waitress retreated towards the bar.

She was revealing a knack for asking unexpected questions. It took him a moment to realize that she was referring to her driving. 'I trust you,' he said. 'But I'm never comfortable, being driven in my own car. That takes a lot of trust.'

'I guess it does. I wouldn't know. Men seem to enjoy a closer rapport with their vehicles than women do.'

They nursed their drinks. Hazel decided that Jeremy had been right. The familiar shop and workshop had been transformed by being thrown together and the addition of slick panelling, junk ornamentation, well-chosen furniture and gentle lighting into something far removed from the utilitarian past. The waitresses tidied around them and were on the point of departure, leaving on only a single light over their table, when Mr Carmichael arrived in the company of a small blonde woman. They saw him settle her in a chair near the door before approaching their table.

Jeremy rose and offered his hand but the bookseller

seemed too distrait to notice it. He forced a smile for Hazel, settled on the edge of a spare chair and said, 'Oh dear! I hope I'm doing the right thing. I wanted you to meet that lady. She's another with good cause to hate Gordon McKennerty. She may be able to help you. I've impressed on her that my name must never be mentioned. If McKennerty ever finds out that you've met, make up some story but – please – leave me out of it.'

'All right,' Jeremy said. 'We'll do that.'

'Of course we will,' Hazel said. 'But, so that we can get our story straight, how do you come to know her?'

'I've been to McKennerty's house many times. Not eagerly, I assure you, but when he says "Come", I come.'

'Why are you so afraid of him?' Hazel asked.

The bookseller passed a hand over his face as if to brush away a cobweb. 'He's a terrible man. I've told Mr Carpenter some of it. Not all, but some. Or speak to the lady, she'll tell you. I'll let her introduce herself.' Without another word, he got to his feet and hurried with nervous steps across the room. They saw him speak to the woman. He patted her shoulder and then let himself out into the street, straightening his shoulders as if shedding a weight of apprehension.

The woman seemed afraid to make a decision. Jeremy thought that she was on the point of following the bookseller out of the wine-bar. Suddenly he saw a reason behind Mr Carmichael's suggestion that Hazel come with him. 'You go to her,' he said. 'She might be afraid of a strange man. Bring her back here, away from the street.'

Hazel nodded, rose and walked the length of the room. He saw her settle beside the woman and speak gently to her. Rather than intimidate the woman by staring at her, he looked away, studying a bogus map of the Scottish clans and tartans. When he looked back, they were approaching. He rose.

'This is Glynis,' Hazel said. Glynis offered her hand and almost jerked it back out of his.

'Do sit,' Jeremy said. 'And tell us why you're here.'

Glynis looked searchingly from Jeremy to Hazel and back again, her fingers moving restlessly. She passed a pink tongue between her lips. She was round-faced and roundly figured but, aided by full lips and the eyes of a soulful spaniel, she still managed to exude an air of sexual attractiveness. She was inexpensively but tastefully dressed, Jeremy thought, but carefully made up although the makeup only went part-way towards hiding the fact that she was older than the first impression suggested. Her hair was fair and he could see no trace of darkening at the roots. 'Alec said—' She broke off. 'Alec Carmichael. He told me that Gordon – Gordon McKennerty – ripped you off. More than that, Alec reckoned that you were going to get back at him by recovering your money. Was he right?' Her voice had a trace of Edinburgh's worst, over-genteel accent.

Jeremy thought quickly. Had McKennerty already got wind of their activity and was this an immediate countermove? Nobody but Carmichael had an inkling of their intention, except that this woman was now involved. Carmichael was too genuine to be part of a plot. Nevertheless, he would move with care. 'Do you know who I am?' he asked.

She shook her blonde head slowly, eyes wide. 'Only what Alec told me. Somebody who did business with Gordon and got their fingers burned. That could mean anybody. Anybody at all.'

'What Alec Carmichael told you was true,' Jeremy said. 'Mr McKennerty swindled me and he cost this lady her livelihood. If we can take him for a lot of money, we will.'

Hazel let a small sound of impatience escape her. 'More than that,' she said. 'To line his own pocket, or increase his own store of treasures, he destroyed a good business which several people depended on for their livings. The owner, my employer, was the kindest man alive and he was left with nothing. He killed himself. We don't want to let Mr McKennerty get away with that. We want to hit him everywhere that it hurts. We have something brewing. We may not go ahead with it, depending on how sure-fire it looks, but at the moment the signs are good.'

Jeremy gave her a warning glance. 'And that's all I think we should say,' he said firmly, 'until we know who you are.'

Glynis hesitated, looking again from one to the other. 'Swear that this is between ourselves?'

'Definitely,' Jeremy said.

Hazel said, 'We swear.'

'Well, why not?' Glynis took a deep breath and let it out slowly. 'I've to trust somebody some day. It's just been such a hell of a time . . . Please, please remember that if you break faith it could be the end of me. Most people would call me Mrs McKennerty. But I'm not. He had me move in with him, nearly twenty years ago when I was just seventeen. We were going to be married, he said, but it never happened. That's how it is with him. If he offers you a penny for your thought, get the penny off him before you tell him. But I suppose you've found that out for yourselves.' She sighed. 'He was good to me at first.

'After nearly ten years, I had a baby, a boy. For a while, Gordon was over the moon. He cared about having a son more than anything. It was as if he loved me again, for a while. Then little Neil had an accident and damaged his spine and his head. He was in a coma for months. It was more Gordon's fault than mine – I was out of the room and Gordon let Neil climb on things. He fell against the hearth. From then on, Neil was physically handicapped, and mentally as well.

'From that moment, Gordon's attitude changed. It was as if I'd given birth to a monster. I became no more than a servant. No, less than a servant, a prostitute. I was there to serve his needs.' Her voice sank to a whisper. 'And his friends'.'

Jeremy was deeply shocked. His studies of history had revealed many examples of that kind of exploitation but he had thought that such dealings, if not wholly in the past, were the exclusive province of the lowest stratum of humanity. 'You should have walked out,' he said. Hazel, who had had more experience of the seamy side of life, sat silent.

Glynis's eloquent eyes filled with tears. 'You don't understand. I tried it once. They fetched me back in the boot of a car, tied in a sack and then . . . I couldn't walk for a week. He's very clever at inflicting pain without anything showing. And even if I'd made it, I couldn't have managed with Neil. Gordon said that if I left . . . You see, Neil's in a specialist home. The National

Health works well if you're ill but it's not so hot if you're incapacitated by an accident. I suppose they think you should sue whoever caused the accident.

'Gordon says that if I walk out he won't pay for Neil any more and then God knows what would happen to him. Gordon won't have him in the house. If I could get away, I'd take him with me. He's a darling child and I love him and I just know that he loves me, he's always so happy to see me. That's how I'm allowed to get out of the house.' Her voice broke. She paused and swallowed. 'He needs specialist help. I'd have to have money. It needn't be a lot. I could work.'

Jeremy tried to think of something comforting to say, but words fell short of his emotions. 'Can you really help us?' he asked.

For a moment all animation died out of Glynis's face. Then it stirred. 'Don't you think I could?'

Jeremy felt Hazel nudge his foot under the table. She was nodding almost imperceptibly. 'Quite probably you can,' he said. 'What would you want in return?'

'I want rid of the swine. Or to get away from him. I'll give you all the help I possibly can. Just promise me half of what you take off him. And if he got what he deserves . . .' She lowered her voice to a whisper. 'Could you kill him?'

Hazel and Jeremy exchanged an anxious glance. This was getting heavy.

'We'd draw the line at cold-blooded murder,' Jeremy said.

Glynis's face fell but then animation returned. 'If he was out of the way, say if he went to jail, I could get my hands on some more of his money. Neil and I could start again, somewhere abroad, somewhere he couldn't get at us. We could be happy together. Gordon's abroad for another week or two, but he'll be back and—' her voice broke again – 'I can't take it much longer.'

After only a few seconds of thought, Jeremy saw his next few steps laid out in logical form. 'We can accept your terms,' he said, 'but, for the moment, I don't want to tell you who I am. I trust your good intentions, but if . . . I won't call him your husband. If Mr McKennerty suspected that something was up, you'd crack. Do you have somewhere where you could keep something small without any danger of it being found?'

'Yes, I do.'

'Right. Do you have a mobile phone?'

'No.'

'Wait here for a while.'

He hurried out of the wine-bar. He made a quick visit to the cash machine outside a bank and then to a shop dealing in electronic items. He was back at the wine-bar within half an hour. Hazel answered his knock and let him in. Glynis was watching apprehensively. He sat down opposite her.

'I bought two mobile phones,' he said. He placed a small cardboard box on the table. 'Just cheap ones, but they'll do the job. Keep your one charged up. Switch it off while others are in the house with you, turn it on when you're alone. Mine will be off and on charge by night, in my pocket and turned on by day. So you can reach me any time of the day.' While he spoke, he was referring to the instructions and keying in a series of numbers. 'They'll both be on-line by tomorrow morning. I've programmed the number of mine into yours, so just key in zero-one and you'll

get me. You understand? Call me when you can. I'll
have questions for you.'

'I understand,' Glynis said. She added, in a whisper,
'Thank you. When I phone, what name do I call you?'

'You don't need a name. It will be me.'

'I wouldn't feel comfortable, just in case somebody
else got hold of your phone.'

Jeremy thought. 'You can call me . . .' Some part
of his mind associated the words *golden* and *fleece*.
'Jason,' he said.

Back at the car, Jeremy hesitated. 'Whatever you say,
I still feel that I'm due you money,' he said. 'You're
sure you don't want to look at the shops?'

'I'm not a clothes sort of person,' Hazel said. 'You
know that by now. I never have been. Anyway, I'd
buy all the wrong sort of things. Unless you came
with me?'

'I'd be less than no use. If I hadn't had proof to
the contrary, I'd suspect you of not being a bona fide
female.'

'A classic example of role reversal,' Hazel agreed.
'A man who offers to wait while a woman shops for
clothes risks getting drummed out of the union.'

Jeremy said that he wanted to think. He let Hazel
drive out of Edinburgh. He soon realized that she was
a competent driver and he let his attention drift leaving
her to get on with it.

After half an hour on the road, she sensed him
coming out of his trance. 'So you didn't want to
give away your phone number,' she said. 'But if
McKennerty realizes he's under attack through Glynis,
couldn't he trace you through the mobiles?'

'I paid cash and put the phones in a name that I made up on the spur of the moment. By the time that the money I deposited runs out, this should be all over. If not, I can make another cash deposit.'

Hazel overtook two heavy lorries before she spoke again. 'You realize that we'll have to go ahead now? Glynis is depending on us.'

'That's not a very convincing reason,' he said slowly. 'I can't take everybody's burdens on my shoulders. I didn't cause her problems, I didn't approach her and I didn't promise anything.'

'I'd call that sophistry. We raised her hopes. That puts us under a moral obligation. And we need her.'

'Maybe. I'm not sure how.'

They were approaching a layby. Hazel lifted her foot and coasted in. 'You drive,' she said. 'I'm not happy, driving an unfamiliar car and trying to think about something else at the same time.' They got out and walked around the front of the car, touching hands as they passed.

'You can put the top down,' she said, 'now that I've got a warm coat. I know you're a man who likes to feel the wind in his beard.'

He smiled but ducked into the car. 'We can talk easier with it up.'

When they were back on the road, Hazel said, 'Let me see if I've got this straight. Assuming that I can make a convincing job of the Grail and you can fake a passable letter, the first hurdle is to plant the letter on McKennerty in a way that won't make him suspicious. Right?'

'Right.'

'For that, surely we need a confederate in the house more than anything?'

'It may come to that, but I don't think so. The best I've been able to think of so far is that the letter turns up among a box full of odds and ends left over from the clearing up of the antique shop. I see it being given or sent to him with a note from you, saying that you found the box in the boot of your car and it must have been left there by the colleague who was finishing the clearing up and it's assumed to be McKennerty's property now.'

'Yay. That should work. But you don't want me going near him. He doesn't know my face yet. You'll need me later, because if he sees you he'll smell a rat. Putting that aside for the moment, you want him to catch sight of the Grail in circumstances which will fool him – or, more truly, cause him to fool himself. Yes?'

'Yes.'

'Next after that, you want to get his money off him. Is what's bugging you the idea of handing over to Glynis half of what we can get?'

He shook his head so violently that the car did a slight wiggle in the road. 'Not now. The money's come to mean much less, since you started turning a cellarful of rubbish into sellable goods. I've just been getting angrier and angrier that McKennerty can go around robbing and pillaging like a Viking and getting away with it. More so now that I've heard Glynis's story. I just want to teach the bastard a lesson, punish him so that it will hurt. If that comes in the form of costing him money and half the money comes our way, so much the better.'

'That at least makes sense, even if it's not the healthiest of motives. And don't call your old furniture trash. In – how long has it been? – in six centuries or so, your family has managed to damage and dump in the basement more antiques than the average family could shake a stick at. Moving on, then, he buys the Grail. He does not get a valid receipt.'

'Would he sell it or keep it? You know his reputation.'

'I know his bad reputation. I know zilch about him personally. Glynis could tell you. Mostly, I think he deals to finance living high on the hog; but living high on the hog includes having possessions to flaunt. If he's going to sell it, you want to tip off the buyer that it's a fake. If he doesn't, you want to tell him and break his heart. But, before that, you want to report it stolen?'

'I want to keep my options open. I'd like to drop him in the shit, away above his head. If I can. That bit won't be easy.'

'No,' Hazel said. 'If you set the price high, he'll maybe send his boys to lift it. If they get it, you don't get the money. If they don't and he comes back to buy it, you want to get his money and still report it stolen?'

'Yes.'

'Very tricky. You have to establish that it was stolen, which it wasn't, and that he was concerned in the theft or at least that he bought it knowing it to be stolen.' Hazel sat in silence as several miles went by. 'Seems to me that you're going to need Glynis.'

'Looking at it that way, I think you're right.'

'I know I am. And she needs us, desperately. I had time to talk with her while you were buying those

78

mobile phones. Nobody,' Hazel said fiercely, 'nobody at all should ever be treated the way he treats her. That swine seems to have collected around him some respectable, top-notch friends but also some hard men – not the roughs and scruffs that you'd expect but, like I told you, a bunch of beer-swilling, Rugby-playing toughs who think themselves above the law. At least one of them is under a permanent ban from the Rugby field for being too rough, and you have to be away over the top before that happens. Those are the ones who do his roughing-up for him. He usually lets one or two of them live in the house, even while he's away, and she has to make herself available. She's a toy. And not just for sex.' Hazel paused and then hurried on in a choked voice. 'Just before McKennerty left for France, he and three of his buddies had themselves a party. There were some girls along. Just for kicks, they tied Glynis to the banisters. They had their fun and then they whipped her. And they left her there all night.'

Jeremy was silent. She saw that he was gripping the wheel, white-knuckled. 'You're right,' he said at last. 'We've got to go ahead and take her with us. Nobody should be treated like that.'

'That's not quite the worst of it,' Hazel said. 'If it hadn't been for the kid, she'd have run off and left him years ago.' They could hardly have been more private, but she lowered her voice further. 'She told me what he does with her when they're alone.'

'What?' Jeremy asked in spite of himself.

Hazel was silent while another mile went by. Then she gave a small shiver. 'I don't think I'll tell you. She told me in confidence, girl to girl. It's not the kind of thing you repeat. Besides, it might give you ideas.'

Gerald Hammond

Jeremy wondered whether to say that he would just have to think of something for himself, but he decided that it was not the moment for levity. 'I'm probably happier not knowing,' he said.

Six

The Grail, in its incomplete state, had achieved a condition sufficiently oxidized for covering with the gold leaf. They admired it together in the kitchen after breakfast.

'Which would have come first,' Hazel asked, 'the gilding or the jewels? Or would they have been done together?'

'Assume gilding first,' Jeremy told her. He made a start to the washing-up. 'I've e-mailed a friend who works at the British Museum and he's going to e-mail me some examples of early German script. I can't do much until it comes. I think I'll go and pay my grandfather a visit. Would you like to come?'

Hazel hesitated. 'I'd love to meet him, but I'd better get on.'

'He'd be tickled pink to meet you; and the chance may not be there for much longer. I don't see how much more you can do until the gold leaf comes.'

'Next time. Believe me, I really have enough to get on with. I've got to have some glues ready to try out. They couldn't walk down to the hardware store and buy synthetic resins, they had to make up a mixture from resins, hooves, cooked oils and thises and thats.'

81

'You don't know what they used?' Jeremy asked anxiously.

'I know exactly what they used. I just don't know what they'd have used for gold leaf. I'd be as happy to have the place to myself for a day while I make smells. You've got your new mobile?' Jeremy patted his pocket. 'Leave me the number, in case I want to call you.'

A list of phone numbers was pinned up beside the phone. Jeremy added the number of his mobile. 'You'll have the place to yourself on Thursday and Friday,' he said. 'I'm lecturing those days. And I'll tell you something else. Like it or not, you'll have to buy some more clothes. What you said once before was quite right. McKennerty knows my face but not this address – I was in a hotel overnight when he spoke to me and we met there again when I handed over the bronze. You're going to have to play the chatelaine of the castle. He'd smell a rat if he was offered his heart's desire by a man he'd ripped off the year before.'

'I don't care if I'm supposed to be the Queen,' she said petulantly, 'I can never wear good clothes as if I was comfortable in them and in a place like this he wouldn't be surprised if the boss-lady went around in jeans.' She looked at him through narrowed eyes. 'You may not be able to avoid coming face to face with McKennerty. He'd be quite likely to make an unannounced visit. But he wouldn't know you again if you shaved off your beard and let me clip your hair shorter. And you could let a little more of the local accent come through, the way you do when you're talking to Ian Argyll. There's nothing else unusual about your voice.'

He made no answer but, as they descended the spiral stairs after putting the Grail into the sunshine for the interior to darken further, she saw him look anxiously into a mirror.

Jeremy was away for most of the day. He returned, carrying several large feathers, in the early evening. All the windows were open but there was still a lingering smell of primitive glues. He had used the new phone to call Hazel, so a meal was in preparation. He took a seat at the table.

'You have a long face. Wasn't your granddad pleased to see you?' Hazel asked.

'He was pleased. But I don't think he'll be with us much longer. He's an old man – my mother was rather an afterthought – and he's failing. He fell asleep every few minutes and when he woke up he couldn't remember what we'd been talking about. I told him about you. More than once, actually.'

'Really? I bet that made his day.'

'It did,' Jeremy said. 'He's been nagging me for years to—' He stopped dead.

'To what?' Hazel turned away from her pans and looked at him. She grinned suddenly. 'To get married and ensure the continuity of the line? It's all right. You don't have to go to those lengths. I've never been good at long-term relationships.'

'You've been pretty good at this one so far. This subject is far from closed. I told him all about you.'

'All?'

It was his turn to grin. 'Every warm, wet detail. He loved it. He was a rascal in his youth. And in middle age too. I left him happy.'

Hazel, while not quite believing him, fell prey

to conflicting emotions. Embarrassment was mingled with a sense of pleasure, hastily suppressed, that two men had been discussing her in terms which many women would consider flattering. She made minute adjustments to her pans while she hurried to change the subject. When she felt that the subject had been safely dropped, she turned back again and produced from a pocket an ornate bracelet from which many of the stones were missing. 'Is this a precious heirloom or can I borrow a few stones out of it? I can put them back without any noticeable damage if you want.'

'Go ahead. Do what you like with it. My Aunt Henrietta, who was a scandal in the family during the twenties, was given it by a friend, some said her fancy man, and the stones started coming out almost immediately. She swore that he'd got it at a bargain price because the stones were loose and she wouldn't have any more to do with him. Why do you want it?'

'The original Grail would have been decorated with precious or more likely semi-precious stones. "Encrusted" was what you said, but that suggests that they were stuck on the surface. They'd have been set into the wood and, though you said they'd probably have been looted at a later date, McKennerty will look at it damned hard and I can only make a convincing job of it by doing it. And, to save you asking, pebbles won't do. They'd leave the wrong shapes behind and, anyway, traces of granite or sandstone dust would be a dead giveaway. I only need one or two of each – I can use them over and over. What are the feathers for?'

'Quills. I called on a farmer who keeps geese. If my e-mail's come, I can start practising my Gothic script.'

'You have ten minutes,' Hazel said indulgently.

An e-mail was awaiting Jeremy's attention in the morning and while he was happily engaged in sharpening quills and experimenting, carefully gloved, with holds and hand positions to reproduce the calligraphy, Ian Argyll drove up to the door with the package containing the gold leaf.

There was no doubting that Ian was consumed with curiosity although, out of native courtesy, trying hard to hide it under a veneer of helpfulness. Jeremy joined him in his van, out of the drizzle which had taken over from the sunshine. 'I've a couple of windowsills need replacing before next winter,' he said.

The joiner produced a large notebook and made an entry.

'Ian,' Jeremy said, 'you've been almost one of the family for long enough. So I can ask for your trust and cooperation now. You've guessed by now that I've got something going on and it's very confidential. Some day I'll tell you all about it, but until that day comes it's too secret for anybody to know. Anybody at all.'

'I can haud my whisht,' Ian said stiffly. 'Ye ken that fine.'

'I do and I hope you will. And all your aunts and cousins for miles around. But I want one more thing from you. Quite soon, it's possible that somebody may call at the pub to ask about who's living in the castle. This is crucial. The lady who's staying with me now is my sister, Hazel Carpenter, and she's the lady of the house. If you have to mention her brother – me – at all, he's not often here. Can you put that across?'

'Nae bother, Mr Jeremy.' Ian was obviously mollified

by being admitted even part-way into the conspiracy. 'I'll make sure that Hannah understands.'

'If he comes, try to keep him away from any other locals.'

'Aye. But I'll see they're all warned.'

'He might try flashing money around.'

Ian smiled grimly. 'Don't you fash yerself, Mister Jeremy.'

'Ian, you're a pal.'

Jeremy got out of the van and tapped its roof. He frowned as he watched it bounce down the driveway. So many potential hiccups to foresee.

In the kitchen, Hazel was mixing something at the sink. Jeremy picked up his rough draft, changed a word and then read aloud. 'How does this sound? Addressed on the outside to Gavain Heydring of Tynebrook, who was my ancestor here in the mid-fourteenth century. Dated thirteen forty – in Roman, of course. "From my castle at Henneberg. Cousin, I send you by messenger the casket of which we spoke when we met. This is for your safekeeping. Tell nobody of this. The messenger is of no account and may be disposed of." Signed "Rupert".'

Hazel blinked at him, dragging her mind back from her alchemy. 'Do you think he'll get it?' she said at last. 'Shouldn't you mention Tinnisbeck or something?'

'The name wasn't Tinnisbeck then. Let him do a little work. If we make it too easy for him he'll start sniffing the air. I think that the combination of those names with the word *casket* should catch his attention. Put him on a better scent, in fact. If you think that the wording's all right, all I have to do now is to call up the *Dictionary of Mediaeval Latin* on the Internet and make a translation.'

'It needn't be too perfect,' Hazel said. 'I don't suppose old Rudolph was particularly literate.'

'He could have been helped by his chaplain. But I'll have to take care not to make it too literal a translation. He won't be able to take the Grail away for examination but he'll have the letter in his hands and he can get an expert opinion. The only comfort is that he won't want to let anyone else in on his secret. Oh well!'

By that evening, he managed a translation that satisfied him; and before he left for his lecturing engagements he had managed several drafts which pleased both of them. 'I'm taking the car,' he said. 'If you have to have transport, phone for Dougal McBain's taxi. Anything else—'

'Anything else, give Ian Argyll a phone,' Hazel said patiently. 'I got that.'

'I think there's plenty of food.'

'We could withstand a siege. For God's sake, go.'

'You've got my mobile number.'

'I've got the number. I'll be too busy to use it. You've got the mobile?'

'Of course I . . .' Jeremy patted his pockets. 'It's still on charge. I'll fetch it.'

'I'll fetch it. You make sure you've got your lecture notes and your toothbrush and things. Your mind's too full of that letter.'

'I expect that's it.'

'Am I getting to sound too much like a wife?'

'More like a mother,' Jeremy said. 'I like it. I need a little mothering at times.'

'Go,' Hazel said.

He returned from his lecturing on the Saturday morning, to find that Hazel had lit and stoked the boiler. The castle was warmer and drier than he had known it. She was working on a shining gold box, patiently mounting and removing opals and amethysts.

'That's beautiful,' he said.

'Pity we have to knock hell out of it and dirty it up.'

'It's in a good cause,' he said. 'I've had three calls from Glynis. She expects McKennerty at the end of next week, so she may not be able to phone so regularly after that. She's getting uptight about having him back.'

'She'll have to clench her teeth and tough it out. We won't be ready then. You can't fake centuries of crap in a few days. Well, you can, but it's detectable. You want authentic, I need time. Did I see a sun-lamp somewhere in this mausoleum?'

'My grandfather's sun-lamp's still in his bedroom. You want to get a suntan?'

'I want to age the timber and the sun seems to have gone back to where it belongs, in the States.'

Jeremy brought in a pane of glass from a cold frame and placed it on two tile-battens across the gap between two tables, with a table lamp providing illumination from below. The ink on his drafts showed clearly through the ancient paper. They chose the draft copy which best satisfied them both.

'Dilute your ink,' Hazel said. 'It would have faded a lot in seven hundred years. And once you start a word, keep going. Nothing gives a fake away like stops and starts.'

'Would you like to do it?'

'I've got plenty to do and I don't even understand

the Latin. Your drafts look good. Gird up your loins and go, go, go! I'll age it for you later.'

Jeremy practised once more on a piece of typing paper and then placed the best draft beneath the original paper. His hand moved unhesitatingly and even Hazel, a ferocious critic of her own work as well as his, pronounced it convincing.

'All we need now,' she said, 'is a few centuries of snot and dandruff.'

'I can provide all the snot and dandruff you need,' Jeremy retorted. 'As for time, Glynis can take it on the chin. This has got to be right. And you can take all the time you want if it will keep you here.'

'That's the nicest thing anybody ever said to me,' Hazel said in a small voice. Jeremy thought that she was joking but when he looked he saw that her eyes were moist.

The paper was already darkened with age. They left it in a damp corner of the boiler room to acquire a convincing pattern of mildew spots and then moved it into dry heat until the paper began to crack. Meanwhile, Hazel finished mimicking the effects of precious and semi-precious stones having been mounted and removed from the Grail. A nervous peace descended on Tinnisbeck Castle.

Several days later, the artefact was finished but not yet degraded. The gilding shone in the shadowed kitchen. Jeremy was loud in his praise. 'If you can't find it in your heart to knock it about,' he said, 'I'll understand. I could do that bit.'

'Don't you lay a finger on it,' Hazel commanded indignantly. 'This is the most difficult bit to fake. It has to be done right. There's not that much to show who made something and when. Dirt and wear are much more revealing. You go back to your old history and leave new history to me. I'll consult you when I need advice.'

The Grail was subjected to many dents and scratches and then gently treated with pumice until much of the cedar showed through the gold. When Jeremy nicked himself shaving, the few drops of blood were caught in an egg-cup and, heavily diluted, added to the stains on the base wherever careful study of the folding of the Turin Shroud suggested that faint bloodstains might be expected to show up under chemical and UV treatment. The casket was given a further ageing by sun-lamp and carefully chosen dirt was rubbed into the scratches. Each step was carefully recorded, using Jeremy's Polaroid camera.

They examined the result together. 'So far so good,' Hazel said. 'Now tell me about the window.'

Jeremy looked horrified. 'Oh my God! I'd forgotten about the window. I should have reminded you days ago. All your work on the middle of the lid was wasted.'

'I hadn't forgotten. Whatever you said, I would have done it this way. You said that the window would have been a later addition. Any short cuts might have shown up, in work getting careless towards the edges.' Hazel paused and her brow creased. She was trying to explain to the uninitiated what to her was familiar and obvious. 'If you set out to do a copy, you can fake it; but for a fake to pass muster it has to be an exact copy. Do you follow me.'

'Not really, but I'll take your word for it. It may

have been a painting rather than a window, but we could never fake that. A window revealing the face on the folded Shroud would be in accordance with the various sacred paintings and the views of the modern researchers.'

Hazel's brow furrowed. 'One objection. We'll never get hold of glass of that age. A painting, almost completely worn away, might be safer and easier.'

'Pigments could be almost impossible. On the other hand, can you imagine glass surviving unbroken for hundreds of years in somebody's cellar? Ian can cut a glass oval. You make a rebated opening and insert the glass and bead it in. Then we'll break the glass and remove all but the smallest powder, too small to date.'

Hazel considered the Grail, her eyes half closed, and then nodded. 'This had better work. We're going to a whole lot of trouble, more than the original maker ever went to.' She sighed. 'All right. You go and see Ian while I take a look at the letter.'

She set to with her pumice and the contents of the dust-bag. The letter was folded and refolded and flattened again, each crease in turn being convincingly abraded. They could never have matched the original seal, so the letter was torn and chafed where the seal would have been. By the time that the glass oval was delivered, the letter looked far more than its age. 'What do you think?' Hazel asked.

'It would fool me,' Jeremy said. 'I think it would fool the experts. If it doesn't, we've lost some money and several week's work.'

'A sprat to catch a mackerel,' Hazel said. 'I've wasted time before now.'

The glass was meticulously fitted into place and then smashed and every last fragment brushed out. When the scars had been aged, the pair were satisfied.

'Dirty it up a bit more,' Jeremy said, 'and we'll fake the fire.'

'Fire?'

'Yes, of course. Had you forgotten?' Jeremy opened one of his books at a photograph of the Turin Shroud. 'You see? There's a repeated pattern of scorch-marks. Nobody knows for sure when that happened, but it's generally assumed to have been before the Shroud and its original casket were separated. So we scorch a corner until it opens enough to let heat and soot inside.'

Hazel sighed. 'Give me two or three days and then light your fire.'

'Surely it doesn't take that long to dirty something? It only takes me a few seconds.'

'It would take you a damn sight longer than a few seconds to dirty gold,' Hazel said patiently. 'Gold doesn't tarnish and not much sticks to it. But over the centuries, things will have been spilled on it. Wine, for instance. Blood, sweat and tears, I expect. All kinds of stickiness. I've got to fake that. Then we burn it a bit. Then we rub off any charcoal or soot which wouldn't have survived and we're ready to go.'

'Almost ready to go,' Jeremy corrected. 'There are one or two more steps to be taken. Try not to be too long. Glynis phoned while I was out at the shops. I had to shut myself in the car and even then I had to be careful what I said. She expects McKennerty home tomorrow and she was sounding rather hysterical. I don't think that she can take much more. When light shows at the end of the tunnel, people get impatient. We don't want her shooting her mouth off.'

Hazel made a face. 'I bet! Maybe you could get the letter to him now.'

'Uh-uh!' Jeremy shook his head. 'If I've guessed it right and if the letter carries conviction, it'll take him a day on the Internet to associate Gavain Heydring of Tynebrook with Tinnisbeck Castle. Then he'll be through here in two jumps.'

'He'll want to spy out the land before he makes any moves. But you're right. I'll be as quick as I can, for Glynis's sake, but without giving anything away,' Hazel said.

It was nearly another week before they were jointly satisfied with the appearance of the letter and the Grail. Jeremy had put the intervening period to good use. 'We've got to give him an excuse to make a good offer for the Grail without telling us what he thinks it is,' he said. 'The simple way would be to use the Grail as a receptacle and let him make an offer for the contents. At the same time, I'll try to persuade Carmichael to pass the letter to McKennerty, saying that it turned up in a bundle of old letters.'

'Mr Carmichael may be too scared for that,' Hazel objected. 'After all, McKennerty's going to know at some point that he's been had and he'll know how the letter reached him.'

'You're quite right. So maybe we can revert to Plan A and get Glynis to show him a package which was handed in at the door, holding the leftovers from clearing up the shop. I've looked out all the odds and ends of silver. You'd better come and take a look at it in case I'm giving away Bonnie Prince Charlie's personal back-scratcher.'

He produced a suitably anonymous carton and they descended into the cellar. A large but unassorted collection of tarnished silverware had been laid out for inspection. Jeremy fidgeted while Hazel began a lengthy study. From time to time she made a sound suggestive of contempt or derision and put an item to one side.

'I'll give some of these a clean,' she said, 'and they can go in the box. I'll write a note on typing paper to say that the box turned up in the boot of my car, et cetera et cetera, the way you said. What gets left can stay in the Grail along with these other bits and pieces.'

Jeremy looked doubtfully at the 'other bits and pieces'. 'Could he really use these as a pretext to make a substantial offer for the Grail?'

'They may look like shit now, but these are the things I was going to clean up for you next. Even if we leave them black, McKennerty will see at a glance that they could be worth good money, cleaned and restored. Then it's his job to convince us. This spoon by James Gordon of Aberdeen, from seventeen seventy. About three grand – pounds, not dollars. A toddy ladle, eighteen forty, by Mackie of Ellon, eight grand minimum. The punchbowl, hallmarked Edinburgh, seventeen thirty-nine, eighteen grand, twenty on a good day. So he gets away with around thirty grands' worth of your family treasures. Talking to innocents like us, if we've said that we're not interested in selling, he could maybe up the price to a hundred grand and still keep it believable. It'd be a new experience for him, trying to convince the suckers that their goodies are worth more than the reality, instead of the other way round. Would you settle for a hundred grand? He'd pay more for the Grail, but I don't see how we could swing it.'

Jeremy's eyes were popping. 'Hold your horses,' he said. 'But, remember, Glynis gets half. You're not leaving us much of a mark-up.'

'True. But I've had another thought. That punchbowl represents real money but doesn't look it. Also, it looks oversized to be credible as a content of the Grail which is shallow. I think we put it aside.' Hazel moved the punchbowl to the top of a badly worm-eaten commode and produced a small cardboard box. 'Are these miniatures family heirlooms?'

'Lord no!' Jeremy looked with amusement at a set of amateurish paintings in tinselled frames. 'Some loopy cousin of my grandfather's did them while she was at art school, from photographs of her fellow students. She presented them to my grandfather, with an air of conferring a dukedom, shortly before she died, and he never liked to throw them out.'

'Perfect. We'll include them in. McKennerty can spend time convincing poor, ignorant little me that they're by some little-known Victorian genius who's since become highly collectible. OK. Give me the rest of the day to get the rubbish cleaned up and to make sure that there aren't any telltale inscriptions or coats of arms. Do you have any real old papers, without your own name on them?'

'There are some receipts and things going back to the year dot. And there are several of my great-grandmother's recipes. I tried one or two of them and the results were truly awful. I was saving them to give to somebody I don't like very much. Why?'

'Because if we include some old papers and some less old ones as wrappings and padding, it would make the letter ring truer. A man like McKennerty, you can count on him looking through any papers that turn up in the box. That would be typical of the way he gets on the trail of his acquisitions.'

Seven

'What's so damned urgent that we have to set off at sparrow-fart?' Hazel demanded. She stretched and yawned to emphasize the point, but she was neatly dressed in the same tweed skirt and twin-set, her usual minimalist makeup was carefully applied and, taking his eyes off the wet road for a moment, Jeremy saw that her eyes were bright and alert. Her hair, now that the unsatisfactory perm had quite vanished, was falling into its natural waves and had been carefully brushed. There was even a bolder touch than usual of makeup. To complete the ensemble, a string of pearls was all that was needed but that would have to wait – his mother's only pearls had gone to the bottom of the Norwegian Sea with her. Hazel looked a thousand times more presentable than when he had first set eyes on her. One thing spoiled the picture. He glimpsed her again in the driving mirror. Out of his inexperience came an answer. Her hair was long, and he had no objection to that on a woman, but on either side of her face it resembled the ears of a spaniel and that surely could not be *à la mode*.

'First off,' he replied, 'Glynis phoned while you were beavering away at the silver last night. She's going to phone again but she thought that this morning would be the only time that she could get away to meet us. If she can't or won't help us, I want to see Carmichael and pressure him into falling into line with Plan B.

'Also, I want to see an old friend. I met him when I was a full-time lecturer in Edinburgh. He was in the Department of Electrical Engineering, but in his leisure moments he'd become involved in some Roman excavations. A Roman camp had been found on the north bank of the Tay, prefabricated out of Northumbrian timber and still holding traces of salt water. There's an old Roman road across Fife and the current theory was that the timber had been hauled that way. But that would have entailed two crossings of major estuaries, going across the current each time. The Romans were better engineers than that and, even if they didn't come from tidal waters, they had plenty of colonials who did. They'd have let the tide carry their rafts up the coast, anchoring when the current turned unfavourable. They'd have had to choose their moment for crossing the mouth of the Forth estuary instead of being swept up the river, so they'd have had to anchor off St Abb's Head to wait for the right moment. And St Abb's Head is just where a Roman *pharos* – a lighthouse – had been unearthed.

'Anyway, we did some research together on that and we've stayed good friends ever since. He's still involved in archaeology and he still doesn't hesitate to pick my brains whenever he feels like it. He owes me and I think he could be very useful.

'Next, I've phoned my bank and that cheque's cleared. I've sent off a deposit against my grand-father's expenses and I want to buy him a few little luxuries.

98

'Lastly – at least, I think it's lastly – I want you to buy yourself some new clothes.'

'Well, all right,' Hazel said grumpily. 'But I don't want any more new clothes. I hate new clothes. I can't do anything in them in case I spoil them. I hate possessions generally. They make me feel vulnerable and tied down and yet I hate it when I lose them.'

'You don't have to lose them. In fact, I'd prefer that you didn't.'

'Something always happens.' All the sadness of the world was in her voice.

Jeremy thought of saying that she would not lose her clothes while she was with him, but he decided that the remark could open up too many areas for misunderstanding. 'Nothing's going to happen this time. You're going to have to meet McKennerty at least twice, and he'll be more impressed if you're a different sort of smart each time. We don't want him getting the idea that you're broke and will be grateful for peanuts – the message is that you don't have to sell him a damn thing if you don't feel like it and you won't feel like it unless the offer is life-changing. If the idea of having some good clothes bothers you, think of them as being on loan from me and you can leave them behind if you ever decide to . . . go.' His voice dropped and faded.

'Or if you kick me out.'

'I can't imagine ever doing that. You're here for as long as you care to stay. Unless you turn against me, of course.'

'No way.' She said. She put her hand on his for a moment and then snatched it away. 'Sounds like I'll be around for a day or two yet.' There was a long silence

99

with only the hum of the engine and the thwack of the windscreen wipers to break it. 'Do you mean that?' she asked at last.

Her voice was choked. He nearly stopped the car but he decided that this was not a good time for lovemaking. 'Yes, I mean it,' he said in a matter-of-fact tone. 'I've told you so and I meant it. And one other thing. For God's sake buy yourself some new underwear. Something coloured or frilly or . . . feminine.'

Her mood switched immediately from emotional to amused. 'You don't need any turn-on,' she said.

He gave a short laugh. 'I'm not looking for one. I'm just tired of having to unfold things in the airing cupboard to find what's mine. Every damn thing seems to be white cotton. I nearly tried to put on a pair of your knickers this morning.'

She had a funny answer ready but the mobile phone in his pocket sounded its note. He handed it to Hazel. She listened for a moment and said, 'It's Glynis.'

There was a layby ahead. He pulled in and took the phone. 'Jason.'

Glynis said, 'I'll be able to get away but not until the same time as last time. Same place?'

'We could come closer to you, if that would help.'

'No,' she said quickly. 'We might be seen. The wine-bar again.' She rang off quickly.

'It seems that we'll have the rest of the morning available,' Jeremy said. 'We'll go and see Hugh – my friend – and fit your shopping in whenever we can.'

'Uh-huh. If you really want me to buy clothes,' she said, 'you'll have to come with me.'

'I don't know anything about women's clothes.'

'Except how to take them off. You do that pretty good. Listen, I've got no sense of style. I'm famous for it. If somebody wanted to go to a ball in period costume, my advice would be great, but leave me on my own to buy smart clothes and I'll look like I'm dressed to do stand-up comedy.'

'You could put yourself in the hands of the shop assistants.'

'They'd palm me off with whatever earned them the best commission.'

That was almost certainly true. 'I'll think of something,' Jeremy said.

'You'd better. My mind goes blank when I get inside a clothes shop.'

'I've said it before. If I didn't know better, I'd suspect you of being a man in drag.' He used the phone again to speak to somebody who he addressed as Joe. They would be there, he said, in about half an hour. He waited for a stream of fast traffic to pass and then pulled out onto the road.

They came into Edinburgh through Gilmerton. Jeremy threaded the complex and crowded streets with the ease of familiarity. Just off Leith Walk, he found room to park and he led Hazel round two corners to a shop. The signboard said 'Stafford Security'.

'Aha!' Hazel said. 'I'd been wondering.'

'Sometimes you read my mind a little too easily. Don't I get any privacy?'

'Not a damn bit.'

Inside the shop, a woman assistant was explaining a brochure to a customer. Through a doorway, Hazel could see a workshop in which a man in brown overalls was doing something to a rack of circuitry. Another

101

woman got up from a desk. She infused the proverbial 'little black dress' with an elegance which Hazel could not explain to herself. Her black hair was dressed simply but would have looked good on a fashion model. Her eyes smiled when they saw Jeremy and she hurried to kiss his cheek.

'Jeremy Carpenter!' she said. 'It has been so long. Hugh expects you.' Her accent was Continental – French or Belgian, Hazel thought.

Jeremy returned the kiss. 'Good to see you, Josephine,' he said. 'This is my friend, Hazel. Hazel, this is Josephine Stafford, Hugh's wife and an old friend. Friends call her Jo.'

The two women shook hands. 'Ho!' Josephine said. 'So at last you make a recovery from the hateful Jennifer. I am glad for you.'

Jeremy decided to move the conversation along rather than attempt a reply which could only lead him into deeper embarrassment. 'Do me a favour, please, Jo?'

'Of course. Only tell me.'

'Hazel is American but, in spite of that, she tells me that she has no sense of style.' (Josephine looked at Hazel for a long moment and nodded. Hazel tried not to flinch.) 'You, on the other hand, have style coming out of every orifice.'

Instead of frowning at Jeremy's turn of phrase, Josephine half-smiled and nodded to acknowledge a well-merited compliment. 'So?'

'So, if you could spare the time, would you care to go to the shops with Hazel? I would like her to choose some clothes suitable for the Scottish countryside in summer.'

'For the Game Fair? The grouse moor? The foot-follower? The dog show? As she is but a little more up-to-date?'

'Any of those. A hair stylist, if you can get an appointment at short notice. And . . .' he lowered his voice, 'suitable underwear.'

'Of course. That is only to be expected.'

'Just a minute,' Hazel protested. 'Don't I have a say in this?'

'Of course you do,' Jeremy said. He waited. 'Go ahead and say it. Did you want to do this on your own?'

Hazel made a face. 'I guess not,' she said. 'I'll be grateful.'

'We go now,' Josephine said decisively. 'I take my credit card. You give me yours.' Meekly, Jeremy handed over his card. Josephine swiped it and Jeremy signed the blank slip. 'Good,' she said. 'So I reimburse myself after. *Pas de problème.* Hugh waits for you in his office. Tell him that I have gone for the day.'

Jeremy was hurrying towards the wine-bar with only a few minutes to spare when the phone in his pocket demanded attention. He stepped into a quiet doorway and answered. He half-expected Glynis's voice, to say that she would arrive later or not at all.

If not Glynis, he thought, it would be Hazel. But Josephine's accent was soft in his ear. 'Hazel asks me to call. She will be later. You can manage with the lady, she says. Where will you meet?'

He was not at all sure how Glynis would react, confronted by a comparatively strange man and without

103

the reassurance of another woman. 'Why can't she come now?' he asked.

'Impossible! We are not finished and a small alteration is being made. And there is the hair. Then we must lunch.'

Hazel might have been persuaded, but Josephine's voice left no room or discussion. He decided to give in gracefully. 'Tell her to come to the car at three,' he said.

The wine-bar was already closed for the afternoon. He waited on the pavement. Of course, Glynis would plan to be late, rather than risk having to wait where she might be noticed. After twenty minutes a taxi arrived. Glynis made no move but peered out anxiously, scanning the street for unfriendly observers. Jeremy got in beside her and gave the driver the address of a pub close to where the car was parked. On their previous visit he had noticed that it was open during the afternoon.

'The lady can't make it,' he said. 'We can meet her later, if you like.' Glynis, who had gathered herself ready for a desperate leap out of the cab to safety, relaxed a little, reassured. 'Have you had lunch?' he asked.

'I couldn't eat.'

The driver was speaking on his radio. The window behind him was closed. 'We can be private where we're going,' he said. 'You won't want to be seen.'

She shook her head.

He paid off the taxi. The pub was quiet after the lunchtime rush. Two elderly men were poring over a racing paper but piped music gave them privacy. They took the furthest corner table. Glynis accepted a vodka and tonic – no smell, he realized – but refused a share of the sandwiches that Jeremy bought along with his beer.

'We're ready to move against your ... Mr McKennerty,' Jeremy said softly. 'I'm not going to tell you any details because it wouldn't do for you to show any reaction if any particular words came up. You understand?' (She nodded. Her vulnerability was such that he found himself speaking to her as if to a child.) 'But we're planning to take him for a lot of money and you definitely will get your share. I don't know how much we can get, but there will be enough profit to share with you without feeling it too much. Can you trust us?'

'I must,' she said. 'I can't go on much longer.' Her voice was choked. She dabbed her eyes with a small handkerchief. One of the old men looked across, suspecting a lovers' quarrel. 'I don't know what you want me to do,' she said.

'Not much. Could you keep a secret from him?'

Her eyes opened wide. 'I think so,' she said. 'I have to, sometimes.'

'All right. In the car, just outside, I have a cardboard box with some bits of silver and a set of miniatures. I want you to give it to Mr McKennerty and tell him that a young lady handed it in at the door. There's an explanatory note inside, but you can say that she told you she found the box in the boot of her car after her colleague had finished clearing out the antique shop and it properly belongs to Mr McKennerty. She didn't leave her name, but you can describe her, if you have to, as having dark, permed hair and being thin and a little taller than average. Make up anything you like, but don't make her sound too much like Hazel – the lady who was with me last time. Can you do all that?'

Glynis had paled. She looked down. 'I think so.'

'You have to be sure.'

'I can't be sure. You don't understand. He terrifies me. When he gets angry, he's the devil himself. It isn't just the violence. Once, over nothing at all, he was furious and he fetched my son home.' Her voice broke. 'Without his physiotherapy and things, his deterioration was pitiful to see. Gordon just laughed. I'll do what you like, I'll keep any secret. I can look him in the eye and tell him small lies when they don't matter, but whether I can look at him and tell a big lie when I know that it's part of a plot against him, without my face or my voice giving me away, I just don't know.'

'Not even for enough money to get away?'

'Don't ask me,' she said desperately. 'I could want to with all my heart. I could promise on a dozen Bibles. But if he asked me any questions, I'd blow it.'

Jeremy gave it some urgent thought while he finished his last sandwich. 'You needn't say much,' he told her. 'The note inside would explain it. Could you just manage to say, "This was on the doorstep"?'

'I think so,' she said again, still doubtfully.

Jeremy thought of reverting to his other plan, but the complications of persuading Mr Carmichael to play along and compiling a suitable bundle of letters in which to include the bait seemed to outweigh any difficulty with Glynis. He wished fervently that he had simply left the box on the doorstep and tiptoed away. 'Is the house empty just now?' he asked.

'Yes.'

'Suppose I gave you a lift home. I'll put the box on

your doorstep. You take it in. Then you can say "This was on the doorstep", without telling a lie. Could you do that? The whole plan depends on it. If you want to take your boy away . . .'

'I'm sure I can do that,' Glynis said. 'It would be the truth, wouldn't it?'

In the car, she said, 'I still don't know who you are.'

'It's safer that way. I'm happier, knowing that you can't spill the beans even if your . . . if Mr McKennerty gets suspicious.'

There was a short and unhappy silence. 'I said I trust you and I do,' Glynis said at last, 'but give me some sort of assurance. How do I know that I'll get my share?'

Jeremy glanced down and saw that her hand, on her knee, was shaking. He hesitated but decided to stand firm. 'You said it yourself, you have to trust somebody. Even if you knew exactly who I am, you still couldn't sue me for your share, not without a proper contract or exposing yourself as a fraud and telling your . . . telling Mr McKennerty where you are and all about your part in it. If you don't do this small thing, you may never get your son away, you'll just be waiting to see who dies first. If you do it, and if it comes off, I know that you'll get your share. Either you believe it or you don't. If you're still in any doubt, use your mobile phone any time after three and speak to Hazel. She may be able to convince you.'

Out of the corner of his eye, he saw her take a long look at him. 'I'll trust you,' she said.

It was long after three before a taxi delivered Hazel

and a collection of bright parcels. She hurried to the car. He saw that her hair had been cut and dressed in a style which was not only modern but very becoming and made the most of her natural waves, yet he thought that he would miss the old, slightly unkempt Hazel. He stowed her parcels in the boot. For the new Hazel he felt obliged to open the car door. 'I'm sorry I kept you waiting,' she said breathlessly as soon as they were moving. 'And I left you to deal with Glynis on your own.'

'My fault,' Jeremy said. 'I should have known better than to let two women go to the shops without an armed escort.'

Hazel gave a little sound of mirthless laughter. 'Let me assure you, Buster, that you can let me loose in a shop any time, if you can persuade me inside. Just don't send that Josephine with me – she just has to be the shopkeeper's ultimate weapon. Nothing was going to budge her until she had me fitted from the skin out. I hate to think what we've spent. I haven't added it up but I've brought you the Mastercard slips and you can figure it for yourself.'

'I don't grudge a penny of it, however much,' Jeremy said. *Within reason*, he added silently. He glanced at the slips and suppressed a grimace. 'You've taken some of the discarded rubbish out of the cellar and turned it into good hard cash. I still owe you, and if you want a share of that money you've only got to ask. I see that you're not wearing any of your new wardrobe.' He stowed the slips in his pocket and started the engine.

'Not where it shows. It's too good to wear but I may give you a show and knock your eye out later. Or I may not. Jo made me dump my old undies. She said that they weren't fit for a lady to me seen in – not by a man! She's some girl. Me, if I have to be seen by some man I'd rather it was in my old white cotton than in fancy things that belong in the "Folies Bergère" or the middle pages of *Men Only*. I'd feel like quite a different person and not the sort of woman I want to be.' Hazel paused. 'I asked her about Jennifer.'

Jeremy tried not to jump. 'What did she tell you?'

'That Jennifer was your wife and she ran off with some guy with money and a yacht, taking most of your money with her.' Hazel paused again. 'I'm sorry.'

'It's water under the bridge now.'

'I guess. How did it go with Glynis?'

They were halted by traffic lights. A large lorry was ticking over beside them, its noise hardly obstructed by the car's fabric roof. When the lights changed and the traffic moved off, Jeremy said, 'Glynis took a little persuading. She desperately wants to help but she was afraid that she wouldn't be able to look McKennerty in the eye and lie to him convincingly. In the end, I had to give her a lift back to the house – a big, Victorian house in about an acre of well-kept garden, far too good for the likes of him. I had to wait across the street in the car until she had made sure that she had the house to herself. Then she showed herself at a window and vanished again while I trotted across and left the package on the doorstep. So now, all she has to say is that the box was on the doorstep and if he asks if she saw who left it she can say that she didn't. That way she doesn't have to tell a lie. That seems to be her sort of logic.'

'Seems reasonable to me,' Hazel said.

Jeremy considered the implications of that remark while he threaded his way out of Edinburgh. When they were on the open road, he said, 'Glynis will keep an eye on the waste paper in case McKennerty doesn't read the letter.'

'He'll read it,' Hazel said firmly. 'There is just no possibility that anyone involved with antiques could come across some ancient pieces of paper and *not* read them.'

'It's a precaution. If she salvages it, we can use it again through Carmichael. Glynis will try to give us a ring to warn us if she thinks he's taken the bait and is on his way out to Tinnisbeck. That will give me time to do a vanishing act, just in case. The sight of me might start him thinking.'

'He wouldn't recognize you if you took your beard off. I already told you.'

'You did. But are you saying that just because you don't like my beard? Or because you don't want to have to face up to McKennerty?'

Hazel made a rude noise with her lips. 'Hell, I'm not afraid of McKennerty. Well, maybe I am, but not if I have backup. Believe me, I can lie to a man so's he'd never question it. I should have been an actress. But that beard . . . You keep it clean enough, I'll admit, but it makes me think I've gone to bed with an Old English sheepdog.'

Jeremy was hurt. He had a fondness for his beard, believing it to transform his appearance into the very model of a Border Reiver. 'You have something against sheepdogs? Because I have to tell you that I'm definitely pro-sheepdog. I'll think about it, but we've more need to think about what we do when

McKennerty arrives on the doorstep. Hugh Stafford will be coming out on Saturday.'

'Bringing surveillance equipment?'

'You guessed?'

'You're going to want evidence of what happens. I don't know what plans you've got in your devious little mind, but that much is obvious. What happens if McKennerty arrives on or before Saturday?'

'Impossible,' Jeremy said. 'He'll look into the box and decide that most of it is rubbish. So he'll put it by, to study at leisure. Then—'

'Next year or the year after?'

'That's a risk we have to take, but I don't think so. He'll go through it and find the letter. As you said, he'll read it. He may have to get some help with the archaic Latin, but he can do that through the Internet. He'll probably go back to his sources – he may even try to contact me through the university – to check up on Rupert von Henneberg.'

'I doubt that,' Hazel said. 'You're the one person who might put two and two together.'

'Maybe. At that point, he'll be building up a head of steam. But then he'll have to track down Gavain Heydring and once he's homed in on Tinnisbeck Castle he'll probably make a few enquiries. That should give him my grandfather's name. If he makes enquiries locally he'll get the story that I planted with Ian, that the granddaughter is the regular occupier because her brother's nearly always away. After that, he may arrive at the door, so we'd better be ready for him.'

'He's a bit up-market to go "on the knock",' Hazel said. 'Perhaps he'll send somebody else.'

'I doubt if he'll trust anybody else. The game's too big. He'll probably spin a tale.'

'Which I swallow whole?'

'The perfect little innocent,' Jeremy agreed. 'Right up until he starts talking cash. Then you put the screws on and do them up tight.'

Eight

T hat night, for the first time, Hazel insisted on undressing in the bathroom. She came to bed in an old T-shirt. Jeremy could only put the unaccustomed modesty down to her being embarrassed by her new underwear. Whatever, he wondered, had Josephine persuaded her into? Doubtless in the fullness of time . . . To judge from the credit-card slips, the shops had been raided for Thai silk and Brussels lace. Well, it might have represented the treasures of his ancestors but, as far as he was concerned, it had been 'found money'. Easy come, easy go. Better some piquant lingerie than damaged household goods mouldering in a cellar.

Two days passed by. Jeremy stayed where he could vanish in a trice. Hazel had to be persuaded into her new clothes. She wanted to buckle down to some more restoration work or a little gardening, but Jeremy pointed out that they had moved, for Glynis's sake, at more speed than was cautious. If McKennerty should happen to get going with quite explosive rapidity and make a visit in person, worn jeans and grubby hands would convey exactly the wrong impression of her financial status. Josephine Stafford had been extravagant but she had stuck religiously to her remit. In the chosen outfits and with her new hairstyle, Hazel was the very picture of a

Scottish chatelaine, elegantly casual but smart enough for an informal garden party.

Hazel spent the time on a more thorough exploration of the castle. 'You still got some nice pieces here,' she said. 'I'd have betted against it but your drying-out routine seems to have kept away the mould. When I can take off these fancy duds and get down to work, I'll go over it all for you.'

The third day was the Saturday and it brought Hugh Stafford. Spring seemed to have put in an appearance at last and the day was one which seemed to have been made for gambolling in long grass or rolling among the flowers which were beginning to show. The heather, already striped by old muir-burning, was dusted with a haze of green as grasses pushed through.

Hugh arrived in a dusty but otherwise respectable Range Rover, accompanied by two spotty-faced youths. Hugh was a stout man in middle age with thinning, sandy hair, a bulbous nose and an otherwise beatific expression. He wore a smart business suit and Hazel guessed that his role was to be a supervisory one. While the youths carried in a succession of cartons, he refused a coffee but accepted a dram, seating himself in the kitchen, perfectly at home.

'You told me what you want to achieve,' he told Jeremy. 'You want pictures and sound recordings of any intruders without their being aware of it. How we perform our wonders you can leave to me. Go for a walk or something.'

'You were going to give me an estimate,' Jeremy said.

'You told me that you didn't need the equipment for very long. You can pay for the cables and for the lads' time. If I get the bits and bobs back undamaged in the end, we'll call it quits. Fair enough?'

'More than fair,' Jeremy said.

Hugh produced a folded paper. 'Here's the invoice you wanted, dated late last year.'

It seemed that wherever they went one of the youths would be doing something mysterious and scowling at any distraction. Jeremy sought Hugh out in the cellar. 'We're going to take your advice and walk,' he said. 'If anyone calls, say that Miss Carpenter is out. Don't mention me at all.'

Jeremy carried an old macintosh. 'You won't need that,' Hazel said. 'It's warm out.'

'I might find a use for it.'

The air was soft and the sun was gentle. They went in single file along a narrow path through the heather, which Hazel realized was a sheep-track. It led them along a low ridge, over a brow and down to a calm lochan which reflected the silver birches. There were sedges over the water and a fish jumped, disturbing the mirror surface.

'Rainbow?' Hazel asked.

'Brown trout,' said Jeremy. 'Wild stock. They grow quite big and fat on midge nymphs.'

'Do you have a rod?'

'My grandfather's trout-rod, a Hardy split-cane. I hardly ever fish,' Jeremy said. 'It seems an awful lot of work in exchange for the faint possibility that a fish might fall for the fly.'

'You must be doing it wrong,' Hazel said scornfully. 'Trout know what their food should look like and how it should act. You've just got to be cleverer than something with a brain the size of a pea. I haven't had a rod in my hand since the last time I was in Vermont, but if you get the rod out I'll show you better fish than you get from the shop.'

The first spring weather was too mellow to be wasted in argument. They sat in companionable silence on the coat spread over a bank of heather. 'You're beginning to sound as if you might stick around for a while,' Jeremy said at last.

'Don't count on it,' Hazel said, but she spoke gently.

'You're afraid of commitment?'

'Maybe.'

'Tell me why.'

She lay back in the heather, turning her face away. 'Why do you want commitment so damn much?' she asked, so faintly that he could barely make out the words. 'What's so wrong about just being happy today? That's all that most folk ever manage. You tell me first.'

Jeremy thought back and discovered that it was less painful than he had expected. 'I had commitment once. It was wonderful. At least, I thought it was until the very minute that she went. I was happy, until then. Perhaps I'm hoping to recapture that happiness. Constancy. Knowing that somebody will be there. The right somebody. I don't want to wake up some morning again and find that it's all gone and I'm alone again.'

'You reckon I'm the right somebody?'

'We work well together. We make a team.' He felt his voice becoming unsteady and took a grip on himself. 'We're on the same wavelength. You only need half a hint and suddenly you're up with me and going ahead. I'm happier when you're there than

116

when you're not. Unless you're faking it, we go well together.'

'In the sack? I'm not faking it. You get top marks.'

Jeremy hid his pleasure. 'I didn't just mean in bed, but I'm gratified. So who can ask for more than that? Most people settle for less and get along quite happily. Now answer me.'

She sighed the sigh of one who is very much put upon. 'All right, if you must have it. I was abused, as a child, by somebody who should have been protecting me. Sexually. It lasted three years. I told my mother in the end but she didn't believe me. Happy now?'

Jeremy sat in silence. 'That's terrible,' he said. 'I'm surprised it didn't put you off sex for good.'

'It didn't do that. Maybe I've got a little too much libido. Or maybe . . . There was a shrink I went to once, he tried to tell me that what had happened had left me feeling that sex was all I was good for. That it was all that any man ever wanted from me and ever would want.' She choked on the last few words. 'He helped me see that it wasn't true but I don't know that he ever got the idea quite out of my subconscious. Maybe he did, maybe he didn't – I don't know – but I have to keep telling myself that, whatever I feel, he was right.'

Jeremy leaned back beside her and took her in his arms. She stiffened and then slowly relaxed. 'Of course he was right. I want a whole lot more than that,' he said. 'Don't you know when you're appreciated? Do you want me to talk about love?'

'No. It's much too soon to use the L-word. The bad feelings are still there. I don't know that I could take commitment just yet. Later, maybe. I'm beginning to believe that you may be the one man in the world who won't turn out to be a louse. I don't know what you're offering, but I feel that a ring on my finger might just as well be through my nose.'

Jeremy relaxed his clasp and she moved away from him. 'I thought I could read your mind as easily as you read mine,' he said. 'But now I can't make out what you're thinking at all. If you'd rather have a separate bedroom for the moment, that could be arranged.'

She sat up suddenly and looked down at him. The softness of her expression was new to him. 'Jeremy! That's the most generous, considerate, unselfish offer I've had in years, but it's not necessary. I wouldn't want that. I already told you, I enjoy getting in the sack with you. I don't want to stop.'

'I'm glad. Well, will you commit this little bit? Promise me that you won't suddenly go off without a word. Discuss with me first.'

'I promise,' she said. 'You promise me there'll be no more talk about separate bedrooms. Unless I snore. I don't do I?'

'Never,' he said, not quite truthfully. He kissed her lightly once and left it at that. They sat up and looked at the view across the lochan past the silver birches misting with the first, appealing green of spring towards the distant hills. Rabbits forgot about them and came out to sun themselves. A peregrine circled over the heather, seeking early grouse chicks.

At last, Jeremy looked at his watch. 'We'd better be getting back. Hugh will be waiting to show us how clever he's been.'

'I suppose.'

*   *   *

118

For three more days they were kept in fretful suspense. Jeremy tried to concentrate on finishing his book. He had removed his beard and suffered a severe haircut. He was ready to make a hasty disappearance, but if trapped by a sudden arrival was quite prepared to deepen his voice, change his walk and play the part of a visiting suitor – or a servant, if that seemed more appropriate. Hazel, who was eager to begin restoration of a badly damaged Jacobean corner-table but was forced to remain clean and tidy in case of an unexpected visitation, contented herself with inventorying the treasures of the castle, setting some aside for bringing back into service and planning the next rounds of renovations. The Grail, body and lid, with selected miniatures and silverware, had been photographed and then relegated to a carefully visible but inconspicuous position within the field and focus of a digital video camera hidden on a high shelf within a dusty old carton of empty paint tins. Anything deemed too precious for McKennerty's interest was banished to a secret cupboard in the attic over the kitchen.

The cellphone demanded attention at last while they were at lunch on the Wednesday. Jeremy answered, listened, murmured an acknowledgement and disconnected. He had the eager but anxious look of a lion-tamer embarking on his act before royalty while knowing that one of his charges has toothache. 'That was Glynis,' he said. 'McKennerty only found the letter the day before yesterday. He nearly went into orbit. He's done very little since except pursue his researches by phone and Internet. Now he's booked a room for tonight at the pub. Wants to do a little more homework, I suppose, before making his approach. I'd better speak to Ian again.'

'Shall we go down to the pub?'

'Better not. We don't know when McKennerty plans to arrive, nor whether he has one of his henchmen scouting ahead. I just want to remind Ian that you are Miss Carpenter and that there's a brother who's very seldom at home. I'll have to tamper with the family tree a bit. From now on, you answer the phone.'

Hazel thought that he was shy about showing his newly naked face to Ian. She decided to spare his blushes. 'Do I keep my American accent?' she asked.

'Definitely. If you try to be British and the accent slips, he might start thinking the wrong sort of thoughts. I know that you Americans think that you're classless but it isn't true. Imagine to yourself that your mother was upper-class Boston, a Cabot or a Lowell. She was American and you spent your formative years over there, only coming here when your parents were killed. From then on you can borrow the family part of my *curriculum vitae*. I've told you about it enough.'

'Remind me.'

He reminded her. After he had phoned Ian Argyll they spent the rest of the day rehearsing every scenario that they could imagine for McKennerty's visit. Hazel was becoming more nervous as fantasy receded and reality made its approach.

Jeremy concealed his own fears behind a brave front. 'Relax,' he told her. 'You're a tough cookie.'

'He's a tougher one.'

'We haven't done anything yet.'

'But we're going to.'

'He doesn't know that. And until we do he's got no reason fall out with us. Quite the reverse – he'll be so ingratiating that you'll think he's your long-lost uncle. It's too late to back out now. Think of Glynis.'

'I am,' Hazel said doubtfully, 'but I'm thinking of me too.'

Late that evening Ian phoned back, speaking *sotto voce*. The visitor had arrived, with a companion. They had expressed interest in the locality and in particular the local hierarchy. McKennerty had asked whether any fishing was available through the castle but had lost interest when told about the lochan and had then turned the conversation towards antiques.

'I wondered what car he'd be driving,' Jeremy said to Hazel. 'Ian tells me it's a Porsche. It would be. A quality performance car which doesn't look particularly ostentatious. Just right for a man who loves his luxuries but prefers to stay out of the public eye.'

'What do I say if he asks about the fishing?' Hazel asked.

'Say that it isn't for rent. But he won't. He has the same problem that we have. His story has to be believable and nobody would come all the way from Edinburgh for trout fishing. They might, for salmon.'

She was restless that night. Jeremy, who also slept lightly, was conscious of her restlessness and began to fear that she would chicken out. In the morning, she watched the approach road apprehensively, but when the house phone rang in mid morning, although she jumped, she answered it without hesitation.

'Tinnisbeck.'

She sat down shakily and Jeremy leaned over her. With his ear close to hers, he could hear the voice and picture the stout, overbearing figure and the heavily modelled features. But the strong presence did not make itself felt over the phone. McKennerty was speaking with deliberate gentleness.

'Miss Carpenter?'

'Speaking.'

'Ah. Miss Carpenter, my name is McKennerty, Gordon McKennerty. You wouldn't know me, but I met your grandfather several times in the past, some years ago. We got on very well. I was sorry to hear that the old chap was failing. How is he now?'

'Very well, considering his age, but his mind comes and goes. He's confined to a nursing home, of course.'

McKennerty's voice was slick with sympathy. 'One never knows whether to be glad or sorry. Sorry that somebody is nearing the end or happy that they've had their money's worth out of life.' There was a pause. 'Your grandfather once showed me photographs of some of his antiques. I'm a collector myself and I happen to be in your neighbourhood. I wonder if I might pay you a call this morning? I'm curious to see what the castle still holds and I might even be able to point out some treasures that you didn't know you had.'

'I suppose that would be all right,' Hazel said. Her voice held just the right blend of doubt and interest. 'Would you be alone?'

'I have a friend travelling with me.'

Hazel let a few seconds go by. 'I'm sure that you're perfectly respectable,' she said haughtily at last, 'but you're only a voice on the phone to me. To invite you into the castle when I may be on my own might be considered unwise; but to invite two strangers inside would be rash to the point of madness.'

'I do understand,' McKennerty said. 'I think you're very sensible. I'll come alone. In about half an hour?'

There was a slight tremor in Hazel's hand as she disconnected.

Jeremy sat down opposite and looked at her. He held out his hand and she gripped it hard. 'You did that beautifully,' he said. 'But, honest to God, I don't think that you have to worry. He's using his real name and Ian knows his face. He couldn't get away with any rough stuff.'

'Who are you trying to convince, you or me?'

'Both of us.'

Hazel emitted a grunt of disbelief. 'Don't kid yourself. If he thinks he can get his hands on the Holy Grail, the ultimate antique, would he be stopped by a fear of suspicion just as long as he was sure he was leaving no real evidence behind? You haven't seen how people back away when his name crops up. He's one of those men who believe that if you consider consequences first, you'll never do anything. By reputation, he goes bull-headed after what he wants and worries afterwards about covering his tracks with a little bribery and a few threats and maybe some violence.'

Her evident fear, and in a woman whom he had previously thought to be intrepid, reinforced his own worries. 'It's too soon for him to be offering violence. He might make threats. But I shan't be far away. And if he's alone you can watch him.'

'But suppose he doesn't come alone after all?'

'Don't open the door if he isn't alone. Lock the door as soon as he's inside. I'll be watching. And I have a shotgun. So don't be daunted by his powerful presence. If there's somebody waiting outside, I'll stay outside and keep an eye on him. If you have any reason to feel afraid, show yourself at the staircase window. Or scream. I'll be there, armed and ready, before you can blink.'

Hazel appeared happier. She looked hard at him. 'I don't think your best friend would know you, shaven and shorn.'

'You are my best friend,' Jeremy said.

Hazel produced a tight smile. 'Thank you. But, just in case you have to show up, rub a little flour or talcum into your hair at the temples, to make certain. Nothing ages a man more than a touch of grey.'

Jeremy complied. He glanced in the mirror and saw a stranger. They wished each other luck. He let her see him collect his shotgun from the gun-safe in the small cloakroom off the hall and went out into the sunshine by way of the back door, locking it and taking the key with him.

He had spent a large part of his life in and around the castle, much of his youth without any young companions. He knew the gardens and the land around the castle much better than he knew his own face. When he was alerted at last by the sound of a car on the approach road, he was lying in a hollow on top of a small knoll below the castle. It was a place where he had enjoyed many a secret smoke during his teens. He could feel the sun warm on his head.

Peering through the stiff stems of heather, he saw the grey Porsche top the slight crest a hundred yards before the castle. Choosing a place where a track came off towards the lochan, the driver parked, ready to turn. McKennerty got out at the driver's side, straightened his back and strolled towards the house. Even from a distance, the man seemed to carry his own force-field with him. Jeremy had not set eyes on him for more than a year and then only in very different circumstances. He wondered how he had come to think of the man as merely forceful. His aura was one of absolute confidence that he could force others to do his bidding. Or was this only perceptible to his imagination, fired by Hazel's obvious fears?

McKennerty hauled on the big bell-pull and, after a realistic interval, the door opened. Hazel looked confident and in command. The two spoke together for a minute. McKennerty's body-language had changed. Then he was admitted and the door closed again.

The Porsche was parked facing the castle and nearly a hundred paces away. It looked powerful but understated and functionally aerodynamic, a satisfying piece of sculpture. It was not in the most convenient place, Jeremy thought, for the arrival of a visitor; but from the castle and looking against the sun it would be impossible to see if anyone remained in the car, while someone in the car could watch the castle. He rather thought that he could detect movement behind the reflections in the windscreen. A puff of tobacco smoke confirmed that the car was occupied.

Jeremy decided to move. He need never be more than a ten-second dash from the castle. Slowly, so that the movement would not be caught by the peripheral vision of the watcher, he rolled behind the crest. Then, carrying his shotgun at the trail, he set off through the dead ground. The distance was short as the crow would have flown, but to remain unseen from the castle and the car he had to travel an irregular semicircle until the bed of a dried stream brought him to the bottom of the bank below the place where the Porsche was parked.

During the minutes in which he had been unsighted, the scene seemed not to have changed. The castle looked timeless, as though it would never change. Jeremy waited, watching the staircase window between stems of bracken.

Time dragged by. He began to wish that he had brought a book . . .

A face appeared suddenly at the staircase window, but it was not that of Hazel. McKennerty, it seemed, had thought along the same lines as himself. There was movement in the Porsche. A door was opened and gently closed, a man's feet appeared beneath it and then his figure came into sight, walking silently along the verge.

Jeremy found that his mind was working at an unaccustomed speed. McKennerty might have anything in mind, from mild intimidation to murder. He might even want his minion for no more purpose than to carry away a purchase, if Hazel had accepted an offer. But the summoning of his help suggested that his intentions might not be pacific. Jeremy was ready to intervene, but intervention would be at the risk of rousing a thousand suspicions. McKennerty, at the moment, must be falling for the bait or he would have said a polite farewell and gone on his way without calling up his reserves. Jeremy decided first to try a distraction. If nothing else, it might buy him time to get inside by the way he had come out, to play the part of an inconvenient gamekeeper.

He left his shotgun where it was and stepped up onto the access road. He opened the near door of the Porsche and checked that the car was not in gear. He was immediately struck by the feel of soft leather and the air of quality. He released the parking brake and, as the car began gently to roll away, he closed the door as silently as he could. A moment later, he was back in cover behind his screen of bracken. The man had never looked round.

The slope was gentle and the car was moving at barely more than walking pace, but as it came over the gravel the sound of the wheels made the man turn. Jeremy saw that he was flat-faced, with a button nose but jug-handle ears. Jeremy waited anxiously. His least conspicuous route back to the castle might depend on which way the car went and whether the man went with it. And, little though he liked McKennerty, he did not want the car to be damaged. Whatever was in the wind was not the car's fault.

The car was preparing to descend a bank of close-cropped heather and then a down-slope which ran for miles. The man would have had time to get through the door to the brake; but thought is never quite instantaneous. The opportunity was lost in a momentary hesitation and, following a false instinct, he placed himself in the path of the car and tried to stop it by brute force. The low front of the car made it impossible. The car slowed slightly but he was forced to shuffle back until his heels caught in the grass at the edge of the drive and he tripped and fell backwards. The car overran his legs before being halted by his bulk. Even from a distance, Jeremy heard cloth tear.

The man's roar of pain coincided with the opening of the front door. McKennerty emerged, hesitated and then started forward.

Hazel must have thought quickly. Her voice carried

clearly to Jeremy. 'I hear the phone,' she said. 'Got to leave you to it. 'Bye.' The door slammed.

Jeremy had recovered his shotgun and crawled along the base of the bank, ignoring the lacerations to his hands and knees, to get as close as he could without being seen. Where he was hidden by a clump of whins – old friends from his childhood – he knelt up and took a careful look.

McKennerty stalked across the gravel. Even at a distance, Jeremy thought that he could feel his fury like a blast of heat. Even so, McKennerty was enough in control of himself to keep his voice down and his words bland.

'What do you think you're doing?' he demanded.

An explanation would have taken longer than the other man was prepared to expend. 'Get me out,' he yelped.

McKennerty stooped for a moment and looked under the car. Then, without a word, he opened the door and dropped into the driver's seat. His weight placed an added load on the body beneath. Then the engine fired, the car went into reverse and jerked back. The man's yell topped his previous noises. Rather than bother with opening a door, McKennerty lowered a window. 'Are you coming or not?'

'Help me.'

McKennerty lowered his window further. 'Get in, you incompetent imbecile, or I'll drive over the top of you.'

Somehow, the man dragged himself to his feet and hobbled to the car, holding his once smart clothes together with his hands. He still had one leg outside when the car moved off and turned in a tight semicircle.

McKennerty drove sedately until he was over the first crest. Then, when he judged that he was beyond Hazel's hearing, Jeremy heard his foot go down – whether out of temper or elation or a mixture of both he could only guess.

Jeremy heard Hazel unlock the big door before it swung open. Her eyes looked wide, she was breathing deeply and there was a tremor in her voice. 'I'm glad that's past,' she said. 'I admit, I was scared. I don't know how he does it, but that man radiates evil.'

'You need a drink,' Jeremy said. He led her into the kitchen and searched in the back of a cupboard for a Metaxa brandy, souvenir of his last visit to the Greek islands. She sank into a chair and jumped up again. He poured what he guessed to be a single and a double, added soda and gave her the double. He pressed her back into her chair, took several deep breaths and made his voice as soothing as he could manage. He sympathized with her sentiment but it seemed important to dispel any suggestion of demonic powers before the idea took root.

'I don't think anyone could radiate evil,' he said. 'It's a physical impossibility. Either you imagined it or else you could only detect it because you knew about McKennerty. Otherwise nobody would do business with him. I admit, I found him a bit overpowering when I sold him that bronze. From what you tell me, I know now that he was conning me; but at the time, if he was exuding anything, it was helpful bonhomie.' He paused. 'If you want to cry off, that'll be OK by me. We can let him have the Grail at a bargain price, wait for him to sell it on and then reveal that it's a fake.'

Hazel shook her head. 'I'm scared, I admit it, but I'm not chicken. Anyway, we can't let Glynis down now.'

'In that case, let's have a look and listen.'

She took his outstretched hand and let him pull her to her feet. When she found blood on her own hand, she halted. 'You've cut yourself.'

'I put my hand down on a flint.'

She insisted on cleaning and dressing his palm before they left the kitchen. In the hall, to reactivate the system, she pressed a switch which had been inserted among the light switches beside the outside door. They climbed the stone stair together.

In the principal bedroom, in the bottom of the recessed wardrobe and screened by carefully arranged clothes, an audio tape-recorder was turning slowly. A VCR waited beside it. Jeremy knelt down and set them both to rewind.

The audio tape, when he played it, reproduced the sound of the door opening. McKennerty's voice came through, rich and affable. *My dear Miss Carpenter, so good of you to let me come and see some of my old friend's treasures.* Feet scraped on the stone floor. *A delightful portrait. I don't think that I know the artist, but if you ever thought of parting with it I could certainly put you in touch with a purchaser.*

Hazel's voice sounded firm. *That was my great-grandmother. I would never think of selling it.*

Of course, of course. Do you have it insured?

Only as part of the household insurance.

You really should insure it for at least three thousand.

'He's not far off,' Hazel said.

The audio tape followed them from microphone to

microphone as McKennerty was given a tour of the main rooms. At one point, Jeremy stopped the tape. 'Is he right about that chest?'

'To within a year. He knows his stuff. Pity he doesn't put it to better use. He could make his fortune without ripping people off. Some people can't be bothered with the straight and narrow.'

'They think they can get there quicker by cutting corners,' Jeremy agreed.

'It's more than that. They find honesty repellent, a sign of belonging among the losers.'

The tour brought them back down to the hall.

And that's all? McKennerty's voice was deliberately casual. *I understood from your grandfather . . . Or perhaps some things have been sold?*

'He's sharp,' Jeremy said. 'He's sounding the depth of the financial water.'

There's a cellar. It's been used as a garbage-dump since Noah was a boy. Nobody has the heart to go down there any more.

Just the sort of place where there might be all sorts of forgotten treasures.

Broken, bent or trodden on, said Hazel's voice, *but I suppose we'd better take a look. I've been on the point of calling in a dealer more than once. The cellar would make a good snooker room. I think the key's in here, somewhere.*

'I take my metaphorical hat off to you,' Jeremy said. 'You were right, you should have been an actress. And if you were scared, it doesn't show.'

Hazel was beginning to breathe more steadily. 'You may as well shut the audio tape off now,' she said. 'In about two minutes we arrive in the cellar.'

Jeremy killed the audio recorder and started the VCR, which had its own small monitor, on playback. The screen came alive. Hazel and McKennerty were already in the cellar before the infrared sensor triggered the camera. Considering the poor light, Jeremy thought the digital picture remarkably good.

Christ! said Hazel's voice. *What a dump! I'd forgotten how squalid it was. The junk of ages has been dumped in here and left to rot. I'll just have to get somebody in to clear it.* Her voice had a lighter resonance through the different speaker.

McKennerty could be seen to cast a glance around. His pace checked for a microsecond as his eye passed across the corner where the Grail lurked but his voice remained steady. *You certainly mustn't do anything rash. This cloisonné jug, now. It would pay you to get it restored.*

That's nice to know, said Hazel's voice. The real Hazel said, 'Crap! It's a fake. And he knows it. He was just keeping me talking.'

McKennerty worked his way round the cellar, dispensing advice with the air of one handing down tablets of stone. 'His mind wasn't paying attention to what his voice was saying,' Hazel commented. The man came to a halt in front of the Grail. *These spoons would clean up well,* he said. *But these miniatures, now. The initials . . . P.K.G., is it? They seem familiar but I can't quite place them. Where did these come from?*

From my mother's family, said Hazel. *She was from Boston. Boston, Mass., I mean. She set great store by them. I don't know any more about them than that.*

McKennerty hesitated, more for effect, Jeremy thought, than from indecision. The man was a quick thinker and had already mapped out the next steps in his mind. *I'm in the mood for a gamble*, he said. *Would you take a thousand for the box and its contents? Some of that silver could be eighteenth century.*

'Late nineteenth,' Hazel said scornfully. Her canned voice said, *That's hardly life-changing money, is it? Perhaps I'd better get a valuer in.*

McKennerty stayed calm. *Don't bother with that just yet. Give me a few days to research P.K.G. I may be able to come back to you with something more significant. Life-changing, you called it.*

I don't expect to be doing anything in a hurry. Hazel managed to sound casual.

'Just a minute,' Jeremy said. He wound the tape back and played the last few seconds again. 'See that? He detached a splinter of wood from beside the break and slipped it into his pocket.'

'I couldn't see – he was standing in my way. I guess he wanted it for dating. And that's about it,' Hazel said. 'We came back to the hall. He went up the stair to take another look at that landscape—'

'Showing himself at the window.'

'Same as you told me to do? He came down again slowly and seemed to be wasting time, talking about squat for a minute or two. Then, when he was ready to go, he seemed to be crowding me a bit. What do you think?'

'I think you had him weighed up better than I did. He's a quick thinker. He spotted the Grail immediately. He left his options open. He made an offer in terms which left him free to hike it up later. You made it clear that you weren't going to be tempted by modest sums like a grand or two so he showed himself at the window. At that signal, the other man got out of the car and walked towards the castle, so I sneaked up from behind and let the handbrake off. I admit, I didn't expect half the drama we got, I just wanted to delay things so that I could detour round the castle and appear from the other direction in the role of a neighbour, lover, servant, whatever you cared to pass me off as.'

Jeremy had been talking steadily, hoping to keep Hazel's mind occupied, but she was not to be distracted. 'What do you think he was going to do?'

'We'll never know for sure.'

'You're hedging. Tell me what you think.'

Giving himself time to think, Jeremy wound the two tapes back and removed the cassettes. 'We'll replace these and keep the originals safe,' he said slowly. 'In fact, I'll borrow Ian's video-recorder and make copies.' He got up from his knees and joined Hazel where she was sitting on the bed. 'I'm only guessing. He was calling up the muscle. He may have had some crafty bluff in mind. Or he may have been going to try a little intimidation.'

'After that, if I'd been for real, I wouldn't have sold him the Grail for a zillion bucks. So what comes next?'

'We're guessing.'

'Go ahead and guess.'

Perhaps it would be better to have it out in the open. They would both be more on guard. 'All right. Let's look at it from the viewpoint of a totally ruthless man who's just caught sight of his heart's desire. He may have made up his mind to try intimidation. Help himself to the Grail, rough you up a bit and say, "If you tell anybody about this, we'll come back and kill you horribly." If he didn't believe that you were going to toe the line, he'd have to kill you. He'd have gone back to the pub and told Ian that he came to call on you by appointment but found the place empty. Then they'd have . . . disposed of you and let you be another mysterious disappearance. That's what I think.'

'That scenario carries more conviction than the others.' Hazel gave a small shiver. 'I just hope you're wrong. I don't like to think of anyone that ruthless, especially around me.'

'He thinks he's close to the ultimate possession, the antique to end all antiques, literally and proverbially the Holy Grail. But maybe he was still undecided. He doesn't know how many other people know that it's here. He might have changed his mind. He still has some research to do. He palmed a loose splinter on your blind side. He's going to send it for carbon dating. And the answer he gets back will send him up the wall. Our next move is to get the whole package out of here and let him know that it's safely at the bank. That should pull his teeth.'

Hazel thought it over and smiled suddenly. 'Does your bank have safety deposit boxes that big?'

'Possibly not. But we can think of somewhere. For the moment, just enjoy the fact that he's taken the bait and gone away and that once what he wants is safely out of here he's got nothing to gain by harming anybody.'

Hazel's smile grew wider. 'And where better,' she said, 'to enjoy it than right here?'

'I like the thought,' Jeremy said thickly. They were both riding high on adrenalin, triumph and relief. He toyed with the zip on her dress.

'No,' said Hazel. 'I'll go to the bathroom. Don't start without me.'

Jeremy held onto her. 'But why? Why this sudden modesty?'

'I just feel an idiot in silky, frilly things. I'm not a wedding cake. And I'm not some sort of courtesan. I'm me, a down-to-earth, practical antiques restorer who likes a tumble in the hay now and again. Those things just aren't me. Jeremy, let me go.'

He released his grip. 'All right,' he said huskily. 'Another time. For the moment, forget it. I think we should wrap the two halves of the Grail and take it in to Edinburgh. Alec Carmichael has a strongroom behind his office where he keeps his real treasures and with a little arm-twisting he'll keep ours for us.'

'Let's do just that.'

'You don't have to come.'

'Listen,' Hazel said seriously, 'until that package is out of here and McKennerty knows it's gone, castle or no castle I have no intention of being alone in it.' She looked into his eyes. 'Are you feeling rejected? Because you're not.'

Jeremy laughed and kissed her on the tip of her nose. 'I'll give you every opportunity to prove it tonight,' he said.

Nine

For more than a week, there was no further sign of interest on McKennerty's part.

Hazel was restive. 'He's gone off the boil,' she said, late on the fifth day, pacing round the kitchen. 'He's decided that Porsche handbrakes don't unset themselves. He suspects enemy action and that makes him doubt the Grail. All our work down the tubes.'

Jeremy looked up from his computer. 'I think you're wrong,' he said. 'According to Glynis, he's still like a cat on hot bricks. You carried it off so well that you almost convinced *me*. I can think of many reasons why he'd delay.'

'Name three.'

'Without the least difficulty.' He swivelled the typist's chair round. 'One, he doesn't want to seem too eager. Two, he's doing more research. Three, he's waiting for a lab report on the carbon-dating of the splinter he abstracted. Four, he could be polishing up his story about the miniatures or even faking a valuation—'

'All right,' Hazel said reluctantly. 'Three would have done. So maybe the fish is still on the hook. But I can't wait around in fancy duds for the next year or two. If I don't rescue some more of your debris and turn it back into saleable antiques, you'll have to support yourself, your studies and your granddad on what you can earn giving talks and writing history books. If he does decide to pay us another visit, we'll probably get warning from Glynis, or else he'll phone first and I'll be able to tell him that the goodies are at the bank so we'll have to meet him in Edinburgh. If McKennerty just plain arrives on the doorstep, I can keep him waiting there until I've had a wash and changed clothes.' She smiled more cheerfully. 'Then I can act real snooty and tell him I was having a bath and I expect visitors to phone before coming.'

'I can't imagine you acting snooty,' Jeremy said.

'I hope you never have to see it for real. I'm going to get on with the overhaul. There's a Chinese ivory chess set down there which should finance your research trips for at least one more book. It was in the back of that busted armoire. You don't play chess, do you?'

'I haven't played since I was in my teens. Nowadays, if I expend precious mental energy it has to be on something that will bring in money. Is the set complete?'

'Well, no. The board needs attention. And there's two pawns missing and one seems to have been chewed by a puppy – or by one of your forebears when young – but they could be carved out of the chipped ivory handle of that broken walking-cane. So I'll get on with it?'

Jeremy shrugged. 'Nothing pleases me more than to have somebody else beavering away at raising money for me, but don't get any paint or glue on yourself that you can't get off in a hurry. I'm going away for most of next week. I'm giving a talk in Carlisle to the Historical Society – Lost Treasures again – and three lectures in Lancaster. I'll visit my grandfather again. I'm not leaving you alone here for five days and four nights, so I think you'd better come with me.'

'I'd rather be here.'

'And have McKennerty find you alone?'

With McKennerty beyond the horizon, Hazel had recovered some of her nerve. She stopped pacing and took a chair. 'If he turns up unexpectedly, I needn't let him inside the door.'

'No, thank you. He might catch you outside. On the other hand, Ian's had one or two enquiries about us. McKennerty may be waiting for a chance to come calling when he knows we're not at home. Come with me. It'll add to his frustration if he has difficulty contacting you for a few days. And you'll have a chance to look round the shops.'

She looked at him askance. 'You keep offering me shops. I don't want to look round the shops. I hate shopping.'

'You'll need something a little less tweedy where we're going.'

Hazel remained peevish. 'What am I this time? Your sister again? Your grandmother?'

Jeremy took her hand. 'Not if we're going to visit my grandfather. I want you to meet him. You are my very much valued lady-friend. I am not ashamed of you.'

Hazel relented. She squeezed and then jerked her hand away. 'I'll tag along,' she said. 'But only because you're right and I don't want to be here alone and looking over my shoulder in case that bastard comes calling. He gives me the jitters.'

*   *   *

They left on the Tuesday morning, carefully setting Hugh Stafford's recorders.

Jeremy gave his lectures. Each time, Hazel crept into the back of the lecture theatre. She was impressed by her usually shy lover's fluency and interested in his material, but Jeremy had warned her, under threat of his extreme displeasure, not to ask questions. He persuaded a professor of history, a lady with whom he had once collaborated on a history of the Ottoman Empire, to take Hazel under her wing. The result was a cocktail dress of great charm and considerable cost and the loan of a good string of cultured pearls. Hazel, with her hair newly done, was a success at the university cocktail party following the last lecture, at which she was flattered to receive improper advances from a mildly inebriated university secretary and a lesbian lecturer in biological sciences.

A call came on the cellphone while they were settling in their hotel room that night. Jeremy took the call sitting up in bed. Hazel, discreetly wrapped in her coat, hurried through from the bathroom and sat beside him, putting her ear as close as she could to his.

'Jason?' came Glynis's voice.

'Speaking.'

'I'll have to be quick. I'm not alone in the house but I had to warn you. He's been getting excited. He's even been nice to me.'

'That's good.'

'Yes, but wait. He knows your house is empty. He didn't get any answer on the phone so he checked and he knows you're away. I had to warn you.'

'Thank you, Glynis,' Jeremy said. 'You've done very

well. I shan't forget.' But she had already broken the connection.

Hazel was looking at him, her brow creased. 'And we're not going to hurry back,' she said positively.

'No, we're not.'

'You're giving him time. You want the place to be burgled.' She pointed a finger at him and grinned her sudden grin. 'That's why you wanted an invoice from Mr Stafford, dated way back when. So that, later, it wouldn't look like a set-up. Right?'

'Absolutely right. You're still managing to read my mind?'

'All the time.' She twisted round and kissed him, using her tongue. 'Are you reading mine?'

'Yes,' he said, 'I think I am.'

The nursing home was a former mansion with a manicured garden, set in open countryside. Half a dozen figures, all elderly or infirm, were enjoying the sunshine on seats or pacing carefully between the well-tended flower-beds. Hazel's impression, reinforced by the quality of furnishings in the panelled hallway, was that it was top-of-the-range and that residence there would undoubtedly cost several arms and legs. She felt a sudden sympathy for Jeremy, slaving at his word processor and selling his inheritance piecemeal without retaining more than a bare living for himself.

A stout woman in a nurse's uniform met them in the hall. 'Your grandfather had a bad turn yesterday,' she told Jeremy. 'He seems a little brighter today. He was asking for you.'

'Should I see him?'

She stole a glance at Hazel. 'A visit would do him

good. Just don't tire him too much. You know where
his room is.'

Jeremy led the way along a softly carpeted corridor,
knocked and opened a heavy door. The room revealed
a contrast of furnishings. Alongside the businesslike bed and a medical trolley was a substantial
wardrobe and several chairs of undeniable quality.
There were two watercolours by John Varley on
the walls.

The old man opened his eyes as they entered. His
wasted form stretched the length of the bed and Hazel
judged that he had been a big man before his flesh had
fallen away. Good bone structure showed clearly under
the tired old skin.

After several seconds of obvious bewilderment his
eyes brightened. 'Jerry,' he said. His voice was hardly
more than a whisper. 'Good to see you. And who's
this?'

'This is Hazel. A friend. A good friend.'

A smile creased his face among the wrinkles and he
stretched out a hand. She took it and felt the bones
under the dry skin. There was no smell of sickness or
age, she noticed, but rather of talcum and soap. She
gave the nursing staff full marks.

'A very good friend?' he asked.

'I hope so,' Hazel said.

'So do I. The boy's been in need of a companion
since that damned wife ran out on him. Is he good
to you?'

'When he remembers,' Hazel said, laughing. 'Yes,
he's very good to me. Better than anyone ever was.'

'Hazel knows about antiques,' Jeremy said hastily.
'She's been restoring some of the neglected bits and

pieces out of the cellar. I've had to sell some of them. Do you mind?'

The old man waved his hand vaguely. 'Do what you must. I'd rather not know. Just look after the place. Sticks and stuff can be replaced, but not history embedded in stones and slates and land. After I'm gone . . .'

'It'll be all right,' Jeremy said firmly.

The old man gave a dry laugh and then choked and coughed. Jeremy dried his chin tenderly for him. The friendly eyes, still sharp, turned to Hazel. 'I'm glad to have met you, my dear. But run along now. Have a look at the garden. The roses won't be out for months yet but there's usually a show of spring flowers. I want a word with the boy.'

'Of course.' Hazel took his hand again and then, impulsively, bent and kissed his forehead.

When the door had closed behind her, the old man humphed and said, 'Dare say that's the last kiss I'll ever get.'

'The nurses don't kiss you goodnight?'

The old man chuckled wheezily. 'Don't think I haven't tried them. And don't argue the point, I know when I'm on the way out. She's the one?'

'It's a bit early to say.'

'Nonsense! I could tell by the way the two of you looked at each other. I knew you didn't want me talking about children in front of her, that's why I got rid of her. She's got good hips. The place needs children and someone to take over, someone who loves it. Place needs loving. Been in the family a long time, longer than almost any other place in Scotland. Only sorry I shan't be there to see great-grandchildren running around.' His eyes closed for a moment, then opened again. 'Getting sleepy. No need for you to hang about. Glad to gave seen you both. Now get back to her. Bring her again, if I'm still here.'

'I'll do that,' Jeremy said.

They stayed that night at a small hotel near Carlisle. Each was restless at the thought of what might be happening elsewhere, but they came together in a sweet entwining of warm bodies and after that they slept.

Jeremy put the car along at a moderate pace next morning but, even so, Hazel was apprehensive. 'Where's the fire?' she said. 'We don't want to meet him on the doorstep.'

'No danger of that. If he thinks that his heart's desire is in the castle and he knows that we're away—'

Hazel relaxed against the seat-back. 'You're right,' she said. 'He wouldn't hang about and risk meeting us. He's already been and gone. Let's get back.'

'Slow down, speed up,' Jeremy said, grumbling but amused. 'Do you want to drive?'

Hazel made a secret face. 'Not unless you want me to.'

They drove in silence for a mile. 'Sorry,' Jeremy said gently. 'We're going back to a house—'

'A castle,' Hazel said.

'All right. A castle where we think somebody, maybe McKennerty himself, has been inside. He won't still be there but I have an uncomfortable feeling that he may have somehow changed the atmosphere.'

'I'm tense too.'

The mixed farms and moorland of the Borders went by. Hazel noticed that he was driving more slowly as they neared their destination. She felt a fluttering in her own belly. Their return to Tinnisbeck would signify a new phase in their campaign.

The air was clear under an intermittent sun. Coming from the south, they could see the castle on its rise beyond the undulating moorland a mile before they arrived. There were no vehicles to be seen. In the village, Ian Argyll was getting out of his van outside the pub. Jeremy pulled up beside him and lowered a window, glancing in his mirrors. There was nobody within earshot. 'Ian,' he said, 'no questions, please, but if we don't phone you within half an hour, come up to the castle.'

Ian nodded. 'Your friends were looking for you yesterday,' he said. 'I thought you'd like to know. I could see the grey car from James's farm.'

'Thank you.'

Jeremy drove on more briskly, turned into the drive and parked at last outside the castle's big doorway. The castle looked as it always did, bland and impregnable.

'Do you want to wait in the car while I go in?'

'I'm coming with you,' Hazel said.

She was on his heels as he opened the door, withdrew the big key and switched off the alarm system. The silence and stillness insisted that nobody had been there that day, but Jeremy called Ian Argyll on the cellphone and asked him to hold the line while they visited every room. Ian waited patiently while they climbed the stairs and looked through half-empty bedrooms, cupboards galore, 'usual offices', a grand drawing room and a smaller parlour which had not been used for ten years . . . When they were satisfied, Jeremy thanked him and ended the call.

'Is Ian always so incurious?' Hazel asked.

'He'll be ready to burst with curiosity, but he'll wait until we're ready to explain. It's a matter of manners. He knows that I'd do as much for him. Let's see what the VCR can tell us.'

'Assuming that he didn't find it. Or they?'

'Let's assume they for the moment. If they came here at all,' Jeremy said, 'they've been very careful not to disturb anything.'

The VCR and its companion audio-recorder had been hidden in cardboard cartons which, purposely, were far too small to hold the Grail and these in turn were half concealed beneath a stack of folded blankets. Jeremy's patience failed at last and he tumbled the blankets onto the floor. Hazel re-folded them while he fumbled with the wiring. 'The tape-counter on the VCR shows eight minutes,' he said suddenly. 'That's a relief. If the tapes had been blank and the counters at zero, we wouldn't have known that they hadn't found the recorders and put blank tapes in.'

'Eight minutes?' Hazel said. 'They weren't hanging about.'

'It would only run while they were in the cellar. I'm surprised that it took them that long to see that a four-foot Grail wasn't still there. There's more than an hour on the audio-recorder.'

He wound back both tapes, put the VCR on a chair and set it to play. They sat side by side on the bed again. The little picture came to life with the same view of the vaulted cellar. There were a few seconds of stillness and the sound of footsteps. Two men appeared from the direction of the stone stairs. First came a thickset man with a bullet head, very close-cropped. He walked with a spring in his step whereas his companion, the man who had been with McKennerty on his previous visit, was limping painfully.

'"Them" was right,' Jeremy commented.

The undamaged man headed diagonally away from the camera and halted. *Gordon told us that it would be here*, said the reproduction of his voice.

They must have moved it. Look around. A box about this by that, said the other, gesturing with his hands as though illustrating the size of the one that got away. *With a criss-cross pattern.*

The two small images looked around the cellar. The man with the limp looked inside an old wardrobe with a broken mirror and then came towards the camera. He seemed to be looking straight at it.

'Oh no!' said Hazel.

Don't bother, Bruce, said the other man. *It's a lot bigger than that.*

Then it can't be down here at all, said the man called Bruce.

But Mr Mac was definite. (Jeremy gave a sigh of relief.)

Bruce seemed unconvinced. *Would you believe in a man who wouldn't wait for you to get out from under the car? Backed the car away, damn him. Nearly took my balls off.*

God! That would have been a loss and a half. We wouldn't have known which part to throw away. Looks like we'll have to go through the place.

Let's make sure first.

They scouted around in the cellar for a minute or

two. The man Bruce came to a halt in front of the wine rack. *I could just go a drink*, he said.

Don't be a stupid cunt. Gordon was clear on one thing. Leave everything else exactly as we found it. Exactly. That's what he said and you know what he's like if he's crossed. I'm not carrying the can for you.

He needn't know.

He always knows. So I'd tell him, rather than have him find out.

They left the cellar, still arguing, and after a few seconds the screen went blank.

'We've got all we need,' Jeremy said. 'But we'll just listen to the audio tape.'

The audio tape began with the sound of footsteps on the stone flags of the hall. One of the men – their voices were difficult to distinguish without the visual clues – said, *Can you manage this lock too?* and the other voice said, *No problem – I can practically get my hand inside it.*

There was nothing of use in the rest of the tape, just the tail-end of the fractious argument as they emerged from the cellar and the sound of footsteps and doors as the two men searched. At the very end there was a voice again. *Lock the doors behind us.*

'That's very satisfactory,' Jeremy said. 'I was afraid they were going to mention McKennerty by name. We're going to have to report a burglary to the police but we don't want McKennerty identified until it suits our purpose. "Gordon" and "Mr Mac" will do very nicely, when the time's ripe, but they give nothing away for the moment.'

'And who do I become when the time is ripe? Or do I hide myself away?'

Jeremy thought it over. 'You are yourself. My esteemed lady-friend.'

'Am I really esteemed?'

'Wait until I've phoned the cops,' Jeremy said, 'and I'll esteem you as you've never been esteemed before.'

Jeremy's phone call to the police produced no immediate reaction, but on the following afternoon a plainclothes detective sergeant from Dumfries arrived, alone in an unadorned Vectra.

Sergeant Carroway was lean, dark, intense, obviously in a hurry and not bothering to hide the fact. He first wanted to be shown the point of entry and when he found that there were no obvious signs of breaking and entering seemed disinclined to accept that a burglary had occurred. The security recordings, and in particular the reference to lock-picking, convinced him but, as he pointed out, there would be no point in trying for fingerprints because the video clearly showed that both men were wearing gloves.

'Edinburgh accents, would you say?' he asked.

'Hard to tell,' Jeremy said. 'They seem quite well spoken.'

'I'm afraid so.' His tone suggested that anything might be expected of denizens of the capital city and that for men who lacked regional accents to turn to crime was stealing an unfair advantage over the police.

Jeremy had been careful to photograph the Grail and its contents, with emphasis on the contents. He produced his Polaroid photographs and a carefully edited list. 'Nothing else seems to have been touched,'

149

he said. He sighed theatrically. 'I'd gathered together the last remaining valuables in the place and we'd moved them up here while we photographed them and made an inventory. I already had an offer of a thousand pounds – his tone managed to make it sound more like a million – and like a fool I hung on, hoping for more.'

'Who was the offer from?' the Sergeant asked eagerly.

For the first time, Jeremy let the truth go. 'A man who came to the door – "on the knock", as they say. I wasn't going to sell to a person like that.'

'Not one of the men in the video?'

'I don't think so. I didn't pay much attention to his appearance.'

The Sergeant seemed to be quite accustomed to idiocy on the part of the public. He closed his book and put it away. 'I should get something done about those locks, sir,' he said, 'or your insurers will soon have something to say. I'll circulate the list and the photographs but I don't hold out a great deal of hope. Most of your silver and your miniatures could have changed hands a dozen times by now.'

He hurried away in his unmarked Vectra, taking with him the video tape and the photographs.

Hazel had resumed work on the chessboard and had therefore returned to her old sweater and jeans. She had kept a low profile during the visit of the Sergeant who, she said, had probably assumed her to be the daily woman. 'Which,' she added, 'in one sense I am. And long may it last.' Her smile faded. 'Are you going to make an insurance claim?' she asked.

'Lord, no! I'm not a crook.'

'You are, you know. You've set out to con Gordon McKennerty. He may have been the biggest bastard unhung, but that doesn't make it open season.'

'I suppose that's right,' Jeremy said slowly. 'All the more reason. If the police ask, I'll say I'm not covered.'

'I guess that's best. What happens now with McKennerty?'

'He'll get back in touch. You do not let on that we know we were visited. You tell him that you were so concerned by what he told you that you took the whole boxful to the bank. Then you start turning the screw.'

'I'll enjoy that. I don't have to keep myself dressed up like the dog's dinner, do I, just in case he turns up unexpectedly?'

Jeremy, deep in thought, put up a hand to pull his beard and was disconcerted for the tenth time by its absence. 'He'll phone first,' he said at last. 'In case he doesn't, keep something in the hall to explain your working togs. Flower arranging or dusting would be a suitably ladylike occupation for the chatelaine of a castle but she would certainly wear gloves. So try to keep your hands clean and soft.'

'I'll try, but I'm not very good at it.'

'Try hard. Anything rather than let him get the idea that you're short of cash or into antiques.'

A week later, Hazel was once again becoming anxious. 'He's taking his time,' she said. 'He's gone off the boil. Or has he sussed us out?'

Jeremy gave her a reassuring pat on the bottom. 'Have patience. He won't want to arouse our suspicions by being too eager or turning up too soon after the burglary.'

'We're not supposed to know that we've been burgled,' Hazel pointed out. She served a mixed grill onto plates and brought them to the table.

Jeremy poured wine. 'True. But for all he knows, we may have guessed. He may also be making a few surreptitious enquiries, hoping to establish what sort of sum you'd consider life-changing. He won't want to pay more than he has to.'

Hazel paused with a fork in mid-air. 'How much do you think he'll think I'd think would be life-changing?'

'We could have a sweepstake on it.'

'Don't be silly. Make a guess.'

Jeremy shrugged. 'Off the top of the head I'd say . . . thirty to thirty-five K.'

Hazel raised her eyebrows without other comment. 'If he offers that, do I take it?'

'Certainly not.' Jeremy laid down his knife and fork, picked up his glass and looked at her over the rim. 'Glynis gets half, remember, and we'd be giving him about ten thousand pounds' worth of antique silverware. What he thinks you might think life-changing has little to do with it. What we're interested in is what a keen collector-dealer would be prepared to pay for what he believes to be the Holy Grail, complete with at least part of a provenance. You can't possibly ask that sort of figure without giving the game away, but if you keep on turning down his offers because you don't really need money and you find the whole subject boring, he has no option but to keep inventing good reasons for upping the ante.'

Hazel lifted her own glass and smiled at him. 'We could keep him sweating for months.'

Jeremy laughed. 'It's a temptation, but we have to remember Glynis. Also, when the figure escalates he might decide that he can think of one other option. Kidnapping, perhaps. We'll have to be on our guard.'

Hazel's smile disappeared. 'When you say kidnapping, you mean kidnapping *me*?'

'Don't get too uptight about it. Kidnapping you wouldn't get the goods out of the bank.'

'What do I do if he asks for another look at them?'

'Tell him no. You can't be bothered. You won't be in Edinburgh again for months. If you show them to anybody, it'll be Christie's. That's your best line to take if he tries to lean on you. If he asks for another look, he's trying to get them out of the bank. After all, he's had one good look and, though he doesn't know that we know it, he sneaked a splinter for carbon-dating. Don't worry – he'll be just as anxious as you are. Maybe more so.'

Hazel had to fidget for three more days. When the cordless phone next rang, she jumped and spilled coffee over the chessboard, luckily without doing any irreparable harm to the patina. That caller was only trying to sell kitchen fitments. There followed a period of activity by telephone salespeople and callers unable to dial the right number. By the eleventh call, she had almost allowed Gordon McKennerty to slip to the back of her mind while she concentrated on inserting a replacement veneer which she had already tinted to just the right tone and colour.

The eleventh call caught her at a particularly tricky

stage of the insertion, much hampered by glue which had somehow got onto her fingers. She let it ring until Jeremy quitted his desk and came through to the workshop. The cordless phone was persisting in its electronic demand for attention. He lifted it and remembered in time his resolution that only Hazel's voice would make the first response. He switched it on and held it to her ear.

They could both hear the words. 'This is Gordon McKennerty.'

Hazel had been wrestling with the same fragment of veneer for several minutes while the glue on her fingers became ever more adhesive. At the same time a strand of hair was invading her eye and she wanted a pee. She said 'Who?' Jeremy nodded and smiled. This was the right tone to take.

'Gordon McKennerty,' said the voice. 'You may remember that I visited you recently. I admired the set of miniatures by P.K.G.'

All thoughts of physical relief vanished. 'Oh yes,' Hazel said. 'Hi! Your name didn't register for the moment. How are you, Mr McKennerty?'

'Very well. You're the same, I hope? I'm calling with what I hope is some good news for you. P.K.G. turns out to be Penelope Gordon, an eighteenth-century primitive who's undergoing a revival of interest in America at the moment. An early Grandma Moses, in fact. The interest may be short-lived, so you might be well advised to take advantage of the market while it lasts.'

Hazel moistened her lips. 'I see,' she said.

'Yes. I wonder if I might come and have another look at them?'

Jeremy shook his head violently at her. Hazel looked away. If Jeremy had a fault, it was a tendency to repeat himself. 'I'm afraid not,' she said. 'After you expressed interest, I decided that I might be inviting trouble by keeping them in the castle so I took them to my bank in Edinburgh. They'll be handy there if I decide to dispose of them.'

'Just the miniatures?' McKennerty asked sharply.

'The whole box. It seemed easiest.'

'But this is even better. I'm in Edinburgh. Perhaps we could meet?'

'I'm sorry, Mr McKennerty, but it could be some time before I'm in Edinburgh again. And really, there isn't a lot of point . . .'

'We could be talking quite a lot of money.'

'Really? How much?' Hazel kept her voice flat and dispassionate.

'I've been making enquiries through my contacts in the American market – very discreetly, you understand, but already several urgent enquiries have come back to me through the same channels. They're talking figures around sixty thousand dollars.' McKennerty managed to infuse both surprise and awe into his voice. 'Say forty thousand in pounds.'

Hazel let a few seconds slip by as if considering. Then she sounded, if anything, slightly bored. 'If I decide to sell, I may try the big auction houses first. If I miss the market, I miss it. Those miniatures are heirlooms. They would be interesting conversation pieces at dinner parties.' She winked at Jeremy.

'Don't do anything precipitate,' McKennerty said quickly. 'If you fancy a gamble, sit tight. I'm told that the reason for the present interest is that Penelope

155

Gordon was involved in a scandal, a *cause célèbre*, in her day, involving sex, withcraft and some of the biggest names of the time – one or two of whom may be represented among those miniatures. A descendant of one of them is about to throw his hat into the ring as a presidential candidate. It was all hushed up at the time but now the researchers have been at work, documents have been found, the opposing candidate is preparing to have a field day and there's the prospect of a major film on the subject. If the film comes off, public interest may be enormous. There should be a decision quite soon. So my advice to you would be to hold on.'

'Which is exactly what I intended to do,' Hazel pointed out.

'Exactly. Of course, if the film gets dropped or the candidate withdraws, the interest may die. I'll keep you posted.'

'Please do.'

'To help matters along, could I arrange to have them photographed?'

'I have photographs. I suppose I could send you a set. You'd better let me have your address.'

'I did leave my card with you.'

'I'm not sure that I still have it.' Hazel voice managed to imply that she had thrown the card away as being of no possible interest.

McKennerty sounded unconcerned. 'Do you have a pen handy?'

Hazel listened to the address. They both knew it by heart. Jeremy broke the connection and laid down the receiver. 'He's well hooked.'

She leaned against the bench. She found that her legs were shaking and she could feel the pounding of her heart. 'You've got to hand it to him,' Hazel said. 'It's a good story. You guessed pretty close. I wonder how much he'll come back with next time.'

'You'll know in about – what? – perhaps a fortnight. He's got to allow a credible interval. One during which you could imagine interest building, but not long enough for you to start making your own enquiries. Then . . . you mentioned a hundred grand once and I could believe in that.'

'Wow! Then do I accept it?'

'We'll see when the time comes,' Jeremy said. He put his arms round her from behind. 'We don't want to push him too far. He might get drastic again.'

'Yeah. We wouldn't want that. And now, to the next item of business.' She raised her hand. The chessboard rose with it. 'Help me get unstuck from this goddam thing. I need a pee. Do we send him photographs?'

Jeremy considered. 'I'm tempted to tease him a bit further by not bothering, but on the whole I'd register mild interest by sending them. Just the miniatures – as far as we're supposed to be concerned, that's all he's interested in.'

Hazel grinned mischievously. 'We could twist his tail for him by offering to sell him the miniatures and nothing else. See what kind of story he comes up with this time.'

Jeremy shook his head. 'It's a temptation, but we don't want to start him thinking.'

Jeremy's guess turned out to be a slight underesti-mate. It was nearly three weeks before McKennerty phoned again.

During that period, Glynis phoned twice seeking

reassurance; but she said that her husband was fretting impatiently and only restraining himself with an effort. His stress had been reflected in resumed maltreatment of herself, but when she was reassured that McKennerty's frustration was a sign that their plans were coming to fruition she declared herself able to endure for as long as was necessary.

'I try not to think about what she's going through,' Hazel said. 'It must be awful.'

Jeremy nodded sombrely. 'But there must be a million people in the world at any one time with just as big problems,' he said. 'Unless you're a saint, you can't suffer for them all.'

'It makes it worse when it's someone you know.'

'Of course.' Rather than seem heartless, Jeremy allowed a decent interval to pass. 'You know, I'm just as concerned with what we do when he comes up with a realistic offer. We may want to move quickly in case he smells a rat. It's time that we opened a couple of bank accounts, one for you in your current name and one for Glynis.'

'Won't they want all sorts of references and proofs of identity?'

'Not now. Most of that went by the board when telephone banking came in.'

It took six phone calls to find a branch bank in Tolcross with strongroom facilities for a package the size of a very large suitcase. Glynis phoned that evening. They made a special trip to Edinburgh in order to get her signature, open the accounts and move the Grail to its new repository.

'This car knows its own way to Edinburgh by now,' Hazel said.

*   *   *

Two weeks went by. They comforted each other with word-pictures of Gordon McKennerty fizzling with impatience and only restraining himself, for the sake of verisimilitude, with an effort that left him seeing spots. As the third week dragged past, they began to believe that McKennerty had seen through their stratagems.

With so much hanging in the balance, Hazel found it difficult to concentrate on the minutiae of antiques restoration and Jeremy, who was in the concluding stages of his newest book, was quite unable to string words together into coherent sentences. On the Thursday, they declared a holiday and went fishing. The tranquillity of the lochan and the battle of wits with the resident trout chased away all thoughts of fear and revenge. With five in the bag – the largest, Jeremy's, nearly two and a half pounds of brightly spotted trout – they found themselves relaxed. The euphoria of a beautiful day, happy companionship and a successful pursuit generated the mood. They could see for miles but nobody could see them. They made slow and beautiful love among the heather.

Hunger broke the mood at last. They walked slowly back towards the castle. As their path crested the last rise, they saw a grey Porsche parked beside Jeremy's car on the gravel.

'Christ!' said Hazel.

'Stay cool,' Jeremy hissed. 'Don't show any alarm. Walk on and keep your body-language calm. He may be watching you. He can't possibly be planning any rough stuff as long as he thinks the goods are in a bank vault.'

Hazel ran her fingers through her hair and then shook her head. Her new hairstyle fell naturally back into place. 'I'm not dressed for receiving that sort of visitor.'

'You've been fishing, for God's sake. No sane person goes fishing in good clothes, especially on their own water and miles out in the country. Carry it off. I'll go in by the back door. Remember, I'm your manservant.'

He adopted a slight limp and lowered his shoulders slightly. That, he thought, should be enough to prevent any sudden recognition alerting McKennerty. As they neared the castle he touched his cap and turned away towards the back door. Hazel, carrying the rod over her shoulder, rounded the corner of the building. She raised her eyebrows in polite surprise at seeing Gordon McKennerty leaning against his Porsche. He seemed to be unaccompanied.

'What a handsome car!' she remarked casually. 'Mr – um – McKennerty, isn't it? What brings you here?'

'I have some news for you. I did try to phone, but without getting an answer. Perhaps I misdialled. Did you have any luck?'

'Luck?'

McKennerty glanced down at the rod in her hands. 'Fishing,' he said.

Hazel smiled. 'Five good ones. But my ghillie caught two of them. It's too nice a day for sitting inside. Take a seat on the wall for a minute while I wash my hands and put this rod away. I'll bring out a couple of cushions.'

Jeremy was waiting in the hall. He took the rod from her. Hazel hurried into the kitchen and began

Grail For Sale

scrubbing at her hands. The window, like all the others, was open.

'I can hear perfectly from here,' Jeremy said softly. 'I'll know if he's giving you a hard time. If you hear me clattering pots and pans, I'm warning you to think carefully – or to make some excuse and come inside for a discussion.'

Hazel dried her hands. 'Got you,' she whispered. 'He's come to make an offer. How high does he have to go before I accept?'

'Use your judgement. My guess is that . . . for anything less than a hundred and fifty K, you should let him stew for a bit.'

'Right.' She brushed a quick kiss across his face, grabbed the two cushions and hurried outside. Perhaps sex had been a good idea. She felt far less tense than she would have expected.

McKennerty was waiting by the wall. His attitude was studiedly casual but Hazel sensed inner tension in the man, over and above his usual focus on his own objectives. She placed the two cushions and sat composedly on one of them. 'I love it when spring comes at last,' she said. 'Everything being reborn and the year coming to puberty.'

'That's an earthy but a poetic way of putting it,' McKennerty said. He seemed relaxed, but Hazel sensed that he was making a special effort to suppress his natural forcefulness. 'In the city, I'm afraid, we're not so aware of the changing seasons. Perhaps it's our loss. You love it here, don't you?'

'More than I can say.'

'Perhaps the news I have for you may help you to ensure the continuation of the dynasty. I'm told that

161

the film is ninety-nine per cent certain to go ahead. Personally, I take that with a pinch of salt. These things are always absolute certainties until it comes to tying up the finance and that's when the cold light of day shows up the cracks. The point is that, *at the moment*, Hollywood is talking as though it's as good as in production; and there are some big gamblers among those who've made their millions the easy way. I sent your photographs of the miniatures to a friend in the business and he's got three of the moguls prepared to bid against each other. He's ready to put down cash right now. I daresay that he's expecting to make a few bucks for himself, but he could just as easily end up with his private parts caught in the wringer, if you'll pardon the vernacular. My advice would be to grab the money while it's on offer.'

'You haven't told me yet what money?' Hazel pointed out gently.

'Nor I have,' McKennerty said, laughing at himself in a way which did not quite carry conviction. 'The sum he's offering would translate, at today's rate of exchange, into pounds at just under a hundred and ten thousand.'

'Just for a few miniatures?' Hazel said. Listening, she could hear no clatter of pots and pans.

Out of the corner of her eye, she saw McKennerty flinch. 'Well, no,' he said. 'That's for the whole box of tricks just as you showed it to me. There are a few of the smaller items which would slot nicely into my collection. I'm prepared to make the sum up to a round hundred and ten and you can consider the pieces of silver to be my commission.'

Hazel might have settled for that figure, but the

reference to *pieces of silver* brought Judas Iscariot into her mind. 'And you're not making yourself a little present?'

'Certainly not,' McKennerty said indignantly.

'Of course not,' Hazel said. She paused. 'No,' she said. 'I don't think so. Not without time to think it over. I'm sure you mean well, Mr McKennerty, but if I'm going to part with the family treasures perhaps one of the New York auction houses would be appropriate in this instance.'

There were still no admonitory noises from the castle.

McKennerty looked dumbfounded. (Hazel had been amazed to hear herself turn down such an offer.) He controlled himself with an effort. Hazel was suddenly sure that she could feel a surge of psychic imperiousness flooding out of him, but he only said, 'I think you're being unwise. That would take you longer than this surge of interest may last. You'd almost certainly miss the market.'

'You could make me an offer for the silverware,' Hazel suggested.

He still kept his patience. 'I'm afraid it's all or nothing,' he said. 'I'll be back in touch. I'll bid you goodbye, for the moment.' He shook her hand punctiliously, walked to his car and drove away with the exaggerated care of one who is containing himself with difficulty.

Hazel gathered the cushions and walked shakily into the kitchen. 'You heard? Was I mad?'

'Time will tell. I don't think he's going to forget it. If he increases his offer, even if it's only a matter of pennies, you'd better take it. I have a feeling that

we've pushed him about as far as he's prepared to
go.' Jeremy sighed. 'Like you, I don't give much of
a damn for possessions, but I would kill for that car,'
he said.

Ten

They slept well that night but Jeremy woke early.
He opened one eye, to see one of Hazel's eyes
regarding him from a range of a few inches. He put
an arm around her soft warmth. 'Restless?' he asked.

'A little. I'm wishing now that I'd taken his hundred
and ten K and we'd got the matter over and done with.
It's going on too long.'

'I know how you feel. I'll be glad when it's over and
we can relax.'

Hazel stretched as well as she could within his clasp.
'You too? I could always phone him and say that I've
decided to take him up on his offer.'

'It's a temptation,' Jeremy said. 'But remember,
more dash less cash. He'd find some reason to lower
the price. With people like Gordon McKennerty, you
mustn't show weakness; you've got to keep dealing
from a position of strength. We'll think about it.'

They thought about it over their usual light breakfast.
Jeremy walked outside to think about it some more. He
came back in immediately. 'The car's gone.'

Hazel's first impulse was to say, 'It can't have,' or
'Are you sure it was at the front?' but that would be the
sort of remark which would drive Jeremy up the wall
when he was already stressed. She hung up the dish

towel and walked out onto the gravel. It was another bright day and she had to shade her eyes to look into the distance. Jeremy had arrived at her side. 'I was looking to see if it couldn't have run away down the slope,' she said.

'Nice thinking. But there would be marks on the verge and we'd be able to see the track through the heather.'

'It's been taken, then?'

'I suppose so. I'd better phone the police.'

He reported the theft. They waited. In the early afternoon, a blue-and-white Escort brought a lone uniformed constable, a middle-aged man of considerable bulk and ponderous habit. He accepted a chair at the kitchen table, opened his book and subjected the point of his ballpoint pen to a suspicious glance. He wrote down the names of the castle and of its inhabitants in patient longhand, followed by the description and registration number of the car.

'It was standing where it always stands,' Jeremy said, 'outside the front door.'

'Where it can be seen from the main road?'

'Almost a mile away, yes,' Jeremy said. 'It isn't a *very* main road.'

The constable tutted disapprovingly. 'Was the car locked?'

'Definitely. I'm told that locks don't bother car thieves or joy-riders.'

The constable waited until his pencil had caught up with the dialogue. 'Did you hear any noises in the night?'

'I've been trying to remember,' Jeremy said. 'I certainly didn't hear the car driving off. That would have woken me immediately. If I heard anything else, I must have thought I was dreaming.'

'I didn't hear a sound,' Hazel said.

'Two men could push the car as far as the crest and then freewheel down to the road,' Jeremy said. 'They'd have to be strongish men.'

'Like Rugby players,' Hazel said helpfully.

The constable finished writing and then laid down his pencil. 'I have to inform you,' he said, 'that, following information received, your car was found this morning in the former quarry at Clerkfield. It had dropped about forty metres, so there's no doubt about its being a write-off. The number plates had been removed but, aided by the information in the phone call, we had little difficulty tracing it to you through the engine and chassis numbers.'

The constable paused expectantly. Jeremy, who saw nothing remarkable in the constable's last comments, also waited. It was Hazel who began to suspect an underlying meaning. 'What phone call was this?' she asked.

The constable referred to an earlier page in his book. There was a trace of malicious pleasure in his manner. 'A telephone call was received shortly before your own call this morning. It advised that the car in question was in the Clerkfield quarry, about ten miles north of here. It also stated that you, Miss Carpenter, had driven it there and let it run over what I might call the brink, for the sake of the insurance money.'

The silence which followed was broken by Jeremy's explosive 'Ridiculous!' After a pause, he added, 'May we see your identification?'

Impassively the constable produced a card issued by

the Lothian and Borders Constabulary and bearing his photograph.

Jeremy would have protested further, but Hazel hushed him. 'For a start,' she said slowly and distinctly, 'I tell you positively that I have never been to that quarry, whatever its name was, and I did not drive the car there nor push it over the edge. I do not even know where it is. We were together most of yesterday and all night, not that I suppose that counts for a damn as evidence. Who the hell was the phone call from?'

The constable had begun writing again. He paused and looked up, observing them closely. 'In normal circumstances, we would not reveal the identity of an informant. In this instance, I could not even if I wanted to. The call was anonymous.'

Hazel's face was scarlet. 'I hope that you're not going to pay attention to an anonymous call,' she said.

'We have to pay attention, miss, although we do find them less reliable than when the caller gives his name. Your car is being removed to the police garage. In this instance, we have very little to go on and so far nobody has suffered loss except yourselves.' He reverted to the earlier page in his book. 'I'm to inform you that unless witnesses come forward or other evidence is uncovered, the procurator fiscal will be advised that no further action is recommended. But, of course, if you were to make a claim against your insurance company, that would raise the question of a possible attempted fraud and a more thorough investigation would follow. The remains of your car will be impounded meantime. It will be returned to you in due course. Were there any contents that you would wish to recover?'

Jeremy could feel the heat in his face but he kept

himself under control. 'An umbrella,' he said. 'And a couple of old coats. That's all I can think of.'

'The radio has been removed.'

'It was stolen months ago, in Glasgow. I never listen to the radio while I'm driving so I didn't replace it.'

'Did you report the theft?'

'No. It was a poor apology for a radio,' Jeremy explained lamely. 'It didn't even get FM. If somebody wanted it, they were welcome to it.'

The constable noted the answer. It was clear that he considered it to be a most suspicious circumstance.

When they were alone again, they adjourned out to their seats on the wall, their usual place for deep discussion in settled weather. For once, the panoramic view failed to calm them.

'Who would do a thing like that?' Hazel demanded.

'Who knows you as Miss Carpenter?' Jeremy retorted.

'Quite a few people, but . . . McKennerty?'

'Of course. That's why I asked for the bobby's identification. It suddenly came to my mind that the whole thing might be a scam by McKennerty, but at least the cop was real. Wait a moment.' He went indoors and came out with the cordless phone and his book of phone numbers.

'Who are you calling?'

'First the insurers.' He made the call. When he disconnected, he was thoughtful. 'The voice on the phone asked me if I was sure that I wanted a claim form and whether I'd reported the occurrence to the police. Somebody has already rung them with the same allegation.'

'But how would McKennerty know which company you were with?'

'Their name's on the tax-disc-holder and he's seen the car. That seems to be the sort of detail he picks up on. What's he up to, do you think?'

'Probably a sort of threat,' Hazel said. '"Look what happens to people who thwart me."'

'Yes. Or else he's trying to put you in a financial bind so that you'll need his money. Luckily, he doesn't know who you bank with and he hasn't connected me with you. We're going to need another car and I'm damned if I put up with another old banger. We won't get the money from that table for a while yet and we don't have enough left from the quaichs.'

'There are your grandfather's antiques, the ones from the nursing home that we put into store. You could buy a Ferrari with what they're worth, nearly.'

'I want to keep them if we can afford to. One of these days we'll hope to start refurnishing. Anyway, we need a car now.'

'Your insurers won't pay up for months, if they ever do.'

'Right. On the other hand,' Jeremy said, 'there's only one sizeable motor dealer around here and he's advertising no-interest credit just now. Let me think.' Hazel waited patiently. 'Yes,' he said at last. He phoned his credit card company, endured the usual long wait until an executive became available. When he disconnected, he was even more thoughtful. 'I don't know how much sense you could make out of my end of it, but they've had an e-mail, ostensibly from one of the credit-research companies, to the effect that your credit, and therefore mine, is suspect. You heard me tell him to check the authenticity of it. I'd better call my bank.'

'How would he know where you bank?'

'How did he know which credit card we use? A credit-research company would fax or e-mail all of them and that's what McKennerty seems to be doing. If I want to write a cheque and drive away, the seller's got to be able to phone my bank and be assured that the cheque won't bounce.'

'You seem to have a line direct into McKennerty's mental workings,' Hazel said.

Jeremy shrugged. 'History,' he explained. 'A lifetime's study of the dirty tricks people have played in the past gives you an insight into what they might do in the present or future.' He phoned his bank and asked to speak to the manager. After the usual delay, he was put through. 'Mr Jowett? This is Jeremy Carpenter at Tinnisbeck Castle. Do you recognize my voice? I ask because somebody has been making mischief. You do? Somebody has been circulating e-mails purporting to come from a credit-research company and casting doubts on my partner's financial standing.' He listened for a full minute. 'Then would you please check up on the authenticity of the report and call me back? This comes at a bad time, because my car has been stolen and I don't have enough cash in hand for a replacement. I was going to ask for an overdraft facility for about a month . . . I'll wait to hear from you, then . . . Yes, quite true . . . Thank you.' He listened again and disconnected. 'He sends his compliments.'

'Courtesies come cheap,' Hazel said. 'In my experience, nobody *ever* calls you back, especially a bank manager.'

'I've known him for years. He'll call back. So will McKennerty. He won't want to give you time to sort out your finances. Meantime, we need transport.' He

171

phoned Ian Argyll. 'Ian? My car's been stolen and wrecked. I need something to get around in. Can you help?'

'I think so, Mr Carpenter, leave it with me.'

Half an hour later, Ian's van arrived, followed by a battered Vauxhall Nova driven by a boy who looked far too young to drive. 'It's my cousin Kirstie's car,' Ian said. 'It's due its service. If you have that done for her, she'll be fine pleased.'

'Thank her from us,' Jeremy said.

In mid-afternoon, Mr Jowett phoned from the bank. As usual, Hazel took the call and handed the phone to Jeremy. Jeremy's credit was good and an overdraft would be available if required.

Seconds later, the phone rang again. 'McKennerty,' Jeremy said. He put his ear close to Hazel's. But, for once, his guess was astray. The voice on the line was harsh and metallic with a trace of a Glasgow accent. 'Miss Carpenter? No names, just think of me as a friend. You've had an offer from Gordon McKennerty. I'm bidding against him in a business deal and I'd just as soon that he didn't have that money to call on, so I'm doing us both a favour and warning you. He can be a very unfriendly man if he's crossed. Maybe you've found that out? I advise you, very strongly and for your own good, to accept his offer and close the deal.'

The line went dead.

'It wasn't McKennerty,' Jeremy said, 'but it was somebody singing his tune for him.' He took the phone and keyed in 1471, but a recorded voice told him that the caller's number had been withheld.

'We need cheering up,' Hazel told him. 'Shall we go and buy a car?'

172

'Hold on,' Jeremy said. 'We have transport for the moment. We don't want to miss the call if McKennerty phones.'

'He won't call just yet. It would be too obvious if his call came right on the heels of the other one. Oh, well! Let's have a drink instead.'

She was proved right. It was evening before the phone sounded again. Jeremy turned down the television and Hazel took the call. By then, they had been cheering each other up for several hours. At the sound of the fat and friendly voice, she felt a rush of conflicting emotions. First anger. Then she remembered that she and Jeremy had fired the first shots in the war. But it came over her that they had been answering provocation, that McKennerty thought that he was stealing away a global treasure and that he was fighting a campaign of dirty tricks to win it. A mood of cold reason flooded over her and her course of action set itself out for her. A succession of brandies-and-lemonade seemed to have sharpened rather than blunted her wits.

'Good evening, Mr McKennerty,' she said. 'I'm glad that you phoned. I was about to call you.'

'You've decided to accept my offer?'

'No. If I decide to sell the miniatures, I'll bear you in mind. I was going to call you on quite a different matter.'

Jeremy, taken by surprise, was looking at her as though she had gone out of her mind. McKennerty's voice, when he spoke, sounded half-stunned. 'What matter would that be?'

'I find that I have to replace my car,' Hazel said. 'Joy-riders, you know? It was overdue for replacement anyway. The only car I've seen recently which I really admired was your Porsche. Would you consider selling it?'

There was silence on the line. 'I might,' McKennerty said carefully at last. 'You understand, it wouldn't be cheap.'

'That's no problem. If we can agree on a price, I can have cash for you the same day.'

The silence lasted for so long that Hazel began to worry. If he jumped at her offer, she could only back out by jibbing at the price. But McKennerty must be shaken by her assurance of ready money but wondering if she was bluffing. They were in a poker game for high stakes, but the joker was that McKennerty wanted the Grail . . .

'The car isn't for sale,' McKennerty said suddenly, 'but I might be prepared to do a deal. Suppose I were to let you have it as part of the purchase price for your box of miniatures and silver.'

'I could go along with that,' Hazel said. 'You have full service records?'

'From day one. It was serviced last month.'

'Very well, Mr McKennerty. You can have the box, the miniatures and the silver,' she took a deep breath, 'for a hundred and sixty thousand and your Porsche.'

'Oh, come now, Miss Carpenter,' McKennerty said. There was indignation in his voice but Hazel could also detect relief, almost delight. He, too, it seemed, had been feeling the strain of waiting. 'My car alone is worth around twenty K.' Hazel suddenly knew that the demand for his Porsche had somehow lent credibility to her approach.

'I dare say it is, Mr McKennerty,' she said airily. 'But I'm sure that you have other cars and I'm afraid that that's my last word, take it or leave it. I have some American friends visiting me next week and I had half made up my mind to ask them to get me the best advice from the States.'

'A hundred and forty and the Porsche?'

'I'm afraid not. That really was my last word.'

Now. The chips were down. Make-your-mind-up time. Would he dare to call her bluff and risk losing the Grail? Or try again to beat her down?

'I think we can do business,' McKennerty said. 'A hundred and sixty and the Porsche. Let me have a letter to your bank and I'll uplift the goods and send the car out to you with a cheque.'

He was not going to give up easily. Hazel heard Jeremy draw in a sharp breath. 'No,' she said.

'No?' McKennerty sounded both hurt and amazed.

'Certainly not. I have to be in Edinburgh tomorrow anyway. We'll meet at my bank – you can choose the time. I take it that you can have the money available by tomorrow?' Deliberately, she sounded doubtful.

'Certainly I can. No problem.'

'Very well, then. You can examine the box of tricks. When you're satisfied, you can transfer the money into my account – a "same day" transfer. When I'm assured that the money is safely credited to my account, you can sign over the car and go off with the box and its contents. I'll give you a receipt, of course.'

'So be it,' McKennerty said. 'Eleven a.m.? You'd better tell me where your bank is.'

The call finished a minute later. 'He agreed?' Jeremy said. 'He's accepted?'

'All the way down the line. Now you don't have to go shopping for a new car.'

He pulled Hazel to her feet and began to waltz her round the kitchen. 'You're as brilliant as you're beautiful.'

Hazel stopped in mid-twirl. 'You mean that?'

'Mean which?'

'Both of them. Nobody called me brilliant before. Or beautiful.'

'Of course I meant them. Both of them.'

Hazel sighed happily. 'I think you're brilliant and beautiful too. But no chicken-counting just yet. We'll celebrate when the deal's consummated. For the moment, we'd be better laying our plans.'

When Glynis phoned later, she said that McKennerty seemed to be in a state of almost manic excitement and, yes, he was busy making arrangements to have a large sum of money available next day. Jeremy told her, 'Meet me tomorrow midday at the pub where we had lunch. Can you manage that?'

'I think so.'

'If you can't make it, I'll leave a package for you with Alec Carmichael. It will contain a chequebook. The account is in your name and it should be very healthy by then. What you do after that is up to you.'

Glynis's voice cracked. 'It's really going to happen? You won't let me down?'

'Yes,' Jeremy said. 'And no.'

Glynis disconnected quickly but not before Jeremy heard the beginning of a sob.

They made an early start in the morning, hurried to Edinburgh through traffic which was beginning to thin after the morning rush and were at the bank in Tollcross as soon as it opened.

Their activities over the previous weeks had been focused towards the moment, but now that it had arrived it was almost an anticlimax. Jeremy faded out of sight and kept observation from a shop across the street, ready to intervene if there should be any signs of coercion. But Gordon McKennerty arrived in a large Japanese four-by-four, leaving the vehicle at the door of the bank with one henchman, the one known as Bruce, at the wheel and ready to drive around the block if harassed by a traffic warden.

Hazel met him inside the bank. 'I do not see the Porsche,' she said.

McKennerty was in a conciliatory mode, walking as if on eggs. With his usually haughty manner missing from his body-language, he was not more than a portly man dressed above his station. He produced his mobile phone. 'It's waiting in the nearest car park,' he said. 'It can be here in three minutes. We wouldn't want it towed away. I have the documents here. May I see the miniatures again?'

The package, wrapped in a sheet, was brought up from the safe deposit. It was unwrapped in the manager's office. While Hazel checked through the service record of the Porsche, McKennerty appeared to study the contents with care although there could be no doubt that his concentration was on the container. He pronounced himself satisfied.

McKennerty went to the counter, signed two forms. There was a long wait until the cashier nodded.

The same cashier printed out the balance of her new account for Hazel. It showed precisely the due amount.

McKennerty, looking pained, signed over the Porsche. Hazel scrutinized his signature with care.

Hazel handed over a carefully worded receipt for the money and the car in exchange for 'a wooden box in two parts', a brief description of the miniatures and a list of the silverware. Her apparent signature on it had been written by a member of Ian Argyll's family. McKennerty looked at it closely and seemed both pleased and amused. As Hazel said later, 'He thinks I'm getting away with the money and not giving my brother a look-in.'

The four-by-four had been chased away from the front of the bank by an unrelenting female traffic warden. McKennerty made use of a mobile phone. Moments later, the Porsche came to a halt outside the bank. McKennerty handed over the keys. The four-by four pulled up behind it and Jeremy saw Bruce hurry inside. McKennerty shook hands with Hazel and the two men left, with Bruce carrying the parcel. Jeremy said later that McKennerty seemed to be walking six inches clear of the ground but he was careful to avoid looking at the Porsche.

Hazel returned to the counter and transferred half the money into the account which had been opened in Glynis's name. A chequebook and bank card on each account was handed over.

And that was that. They got into the Porsche. Jeremy drove, very carefully.

There was slightly more drama in their meeting with Glynis. She was in the dark, old-fashioned pub before them, toying with a small pale drink and watching the door with frightened eyes. Her skin looked grey under the artificial lights. Lunches were being served and the place evidently had a good reputation among the business crowd. Hazel and Jeremy pushed towards her through a throng but Jeremy paused by the bar.

'The occasion calls for champagne,' he said. 'But we both have to drive.'

'You go suit yourself,' Hazel said. 'I'll keep a clear head. It's my turn to drive the Porsche.'

'Nice try,' Jeremy told her. In his pocket, he gripped the Porsche's keys for reassurance.

'The Porsche is in my name.'

'For the moment, it's in the name of a Miss Carpenter who doesn't exist. The insurance is in mine. I phoned last night.'

'Swine!' She glanced quickly at the chalkboard. 'I'll have the scampi and just one spritzer to celebrate.' She moved on.

Jeremy ordered the food and bought the spritzer – he had to tell the barman how to make it. He would have liked to order a black velvet for himself but, with the Porsche to drive, it would not be a good time to put his licence at risk. He contented himself with a half-pint of lager. He brought the drinks to the table. Hazel was trying to reassure Glynis. 'You don't ever have to go back there again if you don't want to.'

'God, I hope not.' Glynis lowered her voice further. 'He's got so scary, even more than before. There was a party a week ago. I wasn't there but I know that one of the girls, a tart, came back to the house, complaining that she'd been beaten. She wanted money or she'd go to the police. I don't know what came of it, but since then he's been ready to go for me if I as much as look at him.'

'It's true,' Jeremy said. 'You can put it all behind you.'

Hazel produced the chequebook and bank card, along with a slip showing the balance in the account. Glynis put out a hand as if she expected them to bite. She looked at the monetary figures. 'You're not kidding me?'

'We'd have nothing to gain by kidding you,' Jeremy pointed out. 'We needn't have come here at all if we were having you on.'

'You can draw as much of the cash as you want,' Hazel said. 'Collect your son. Go to the other end of the country. The other end of the *world*. Be happy together.'

'This is his money?'

'Yes,' they said together. 'It was,' Jeremy added. 'It's yours now.'

'Then I can take it and be damned to him.' Glynis put her head down and they saw tears falling unheeded into her lap. 'I'm sorry,' she said. 'I'm sorry.'

'It's all right,' Hazel said. She put an arm round the other woman and Glynis turned to her. Jeremy looked around but none of the other customers was paying any attention.

'I can't tell you what it means,' Glynis whispered into Hazel's neck. 'After these years.' Her small handkerchief was sodden. Hazel produced a handful of paper tissues.

'Are you sure that you wouldn't like another drink?' Jeremy asked.

Glynis shook her head. 'He'd know.'

'But you don't have to go back there,' Hazel said. 'Not if you're so afraid.'

'My passport . . .' Without warning, Glynis began to laugh on a high note. Hazel shook her by the arm and then, when the laughter continued, Jeremy leaned forward to screen them and Hazel gave her a slap. It was not very hard but it had the intended effect. Glynis drew in a shuddering breath and squeezed her eyes shut. 'Sorry,' she whispered. One or two customers were looking, but hysteria seemed to be commonplace to them.

'It's all right,' Hazel said. 'Go quickly. Wash first, in the toilet, or he'll know that something's up. Then collect your things and get out of here.'

'Get rid of the mobile phone,' Jeremy said. 'Or give it to me. I'll do the same. We won't need them again.'

'That's right,' Glynis said shakily. She got up and vanished in the direction of the toilets. When she returned, she was white but in control of herself. She perched on the edge of her chair. 'I'm going to take the money,' she said. 'I don't feel that I've done anything to earn it and I may not even need this much. I feel that I can trust you absolutely.' She took a pen out of her bag. 'So I'm going to leave you a blank cheque. That way, if you ever need money or if I can't use it all, you have access to it. I know you wouldn't leave me broke.' She handed Jeremy the cheque and stood up. 'You won't hear from me again. But God bless you both. I'll think of you always.'

She got up and walked to the door without looking back. The last that they saw of her was of a dark figure against the light outside, squaring its shoulders to face a whole new world.

Their food arrived. 'Another spritzer?' Jeremy asked.

'Nothing for me.'

'You realize, we did it?'

'But it's not all over?'

'No, not yet.'

'What's still to happen? Our part isn't finished.'

'No. If we do nothing, he may make a huge profit; and it wasn't for that that you did all that work. So. Some time in the future, he sells it on. After that, it's up to us. We can tell the purchaser that it's a fake or that it was stolen, or both. And if any of the silver turns up on the market, we can claim it and let the police track it back to McKennerty.' He turned and smiled into Hazel's eyes. 'Half a day to number the pages will see my book into the post to my agent. Just for the moment, I don't want to be asked to authenticate the provenance of the letter and the Grail. I just want to visit my grandfather again. Then I'm due for another research trip. Are you coming?'

'Where to?'

'Somewhere abroad where the Inland Revenue will accept the journey as being for purposes of bona fide research. Whether I do any work is another matter. I owe myself a holiday and we can afford one. You're my secretary.'

'Of course,' Hazel said. 'Your secretary now?'

'For tax purposes.'

'It's a comedown from being your sister. You surely couldn't manage to take a break without a secretary.' She gathered up her coat and scarf.

The cars were parked side by side in a car park only yards away, like a duchess accompanied by a poor relation; but first Jeremy led Hazel down the street to a wine merchant where he purchased several bottles of a moderately priced champagne. Outside again, he said, 'I fancy at least one black velvet to celebrate.'

'You'll get as randy as all-out, drinking that stuff.'

'I already am. It's the relief, I think.'

'Great!' she said, laughing. 'Let's get back home quick before the mood wears off.'

The mood was less enduring that she hoped. Jeremy firmly took control of the Porsche. The day was dreary but it seemed to be bathed in a golden glow. He led the other car to the village and drove another few miles to leave it at the local service station for the forthcoming service; and then allowed Hazel to drive him home. They reached the castle in the late afternoon and Jeremy made what should have been a routine phone call to check on his grandfather's condition and arrange to visit him the next day. But the old man had died quietly in his sleep that morning.

Eleven

'What on earth,' Hazel said, 'are you going to try to kid the tax man you're researching in Brittany, for more than two months?' The couple were at ease beside a small river, in a meadow hemmed in by tall oaks in full leaf. It was a peaceful spot which seemed to be quite unknown to other humans. Hazel was stretched out in a recliner borrowed from the *auberge*.

'The Arthurian legend,' Jeremy said sleepily. He turned over on the rug to expose a different area of sunblock to the sun.

'Like your King Arthur? I thought he was as English as you can get.'

'He was almost certainly Welsh,' Jeremy said. 'The legends were carried over here by the Crusaders and this is where the tales of knight-errantry and jousting and fair ladies got attached later, most likely by the same Crusaders on their way back from the Middle East. Then the legends came back to Britain, apparently with the Normans, and got incorporated into fiction by Mallory and others. A lot of work has been done on the legends, but it's the original Arthur I'd like to concentrate on. If the name has got attached to the right character, he was quite a boy. He was a successful Romano-British guerrilla who held off the

Saxon advance into Wales for longer than you'd have thought possible.'

'Well, bully for him. I don't see you doing a lot of work on him just at the moment.'

'I did most of the work I could think of years ago and I've been saving any material I came across ever since I graduated. Nobody has the faintest real idea where Camelot was, which is worth a little more work some day. I've just been putting off doing it or writing anything. I may decide that the time's ripe for a popular, coffee-table sort of book about him, but I'll more probably come to a carefully considered decision that there isn't a book in it yet and I'll start something else, giving me grounds for another trip later in the year.'

'I said you were a crook. How many men would duck and dive to get their honeymoon before tax? And I bet you're not going to pay tax on what we took off McKennerty.'

Jeremy yawned. 'Certainly not. Disposal of a capital asset. Not taxable. At least I don't think so.' He raised his head for a look around, but they had the riverside to themselves apart from a solitary blackbird in the nearest oak. 'If McKennerty tries to make trouble for me by that avenue, he can't prove a thing. That wasn't your real signature on the receipt and we have evidence that he ordered the theft of the goodies anyway.'

Hazel studied her two rings. They still surprised her. 'I hope we know what we're doing,' she said. 'I can head for the hills if it all goes ker-blooey, but you'll have to stick around the castle and settle your grandfather's affairs. It's a shame he didn't live long enough to hear we were going to get married.'

'He knew all right. He told me. I think that's why he decided that he could let go in the end.'

There had been time for a brief cremation ceremony. The old man's codicil had been quite specific, though worded in a manner which had put years on his solicitor. *I don't want any fuss and nonsense*, he had written. *Just have a memorial knees-up in the castle and let me blow away across the moor where I've been happy.* Jeremy was carrying the ashes in the Porsche, ready for a scattering on their return to Tinnisbeck. 'You're sure,' he said, 'that you don't mind not having had a white wedding and all the trimmings?'

Hazel chuckled. 'Absolutely dead certain positive. You know how I hate fancy wrappings. I'd have looked stupid in a wedding dress and felt a hypocrite in a white one. I can't think of anyone I'd have wanted to have at our wedding, except possibly your grandfather, and I don't think there are more than a dozen that you'd have wanted.'

'If that,' Jeremy admitted.

'There you are, then. I feel just as married even if I didn't understand half what the mayor said.' She returned to her study of a newspaper, aided by a French dictionary. The British papers, if they arrived at all, were usually long out of date.

'Any more in there about the Grail?' Jeremy asked. News and rumour about their artefact had been escalating for several weeks. Not just the Catholic but the Christian and academic worlds had been set abuzz.

'I'm just reading about it. Scientific tests all positive . . .' she thumbed through the dictionary '. . . fully authenticated . . .'

'Not just my brilliant and beautiful partner any more,' Jeremy said. 'Now my brilliant and beautiful wife.'

'Don't stop saying that. It isn't true, but keep on saying it anyway.' Suddenly Hazel gasped and sat up. 'Oh my golly!'

'What?'

'I should have thought of it . . . warned you . . . Come to think, it was obvious from the first.'

'What was?' Jeremy rolled over and sat up.

Hazel had paled under her new tan. 'We were thinking of a private purchaser or a museum,' she said. 'But this could turn everything upside down. Don't you think?'

'I don't know until you tell me what it says.'

'The Catholic Church seems to be buying it. It says here – I think – that the Vatican is putting up the money for the purchase and the price is rumoured to be . . . well, in lira, the zeros go halfway across the page, but because the seller's British it goes on to say that in pounds it's well into seven figures.'

'Great,' Jeremy said.

'*Great*?'

'Yes. The higher he climbs, the harder he'll fall when we pull the ladder out from under him.'

Hazel looked around but there was nobody within earshot. 'You may be listening,' she said severely, 'but you're not taking it in. We've been thinking of McKennerty selling to a private collector or to a museum – comparatively soft targets. The Catholic Church is a different proposition entirely.'

'You reckon?'

'Yes I do bloody reckon.' She turned on the recliner, lowered her feet to the grass and pointed a finger at

Jeremy for emphasis. 'You're thinking of the Church as a congregation of old women. I never told you this, but I was brought up a Catholic. One of my uncles was a priest who made it to cardinal and I heard things. I lapsed a long time ago but I still remember. The Catholic Church may be a religious body on the face of it, but its business interests come very close behind. In fact, I wouldn't be at all surprised if, for many, the financial tail doesn't wag the religious dog. There are some very tough money men at the heart of the Church and some even harder men on its fringes. They have some of the toughest lawyers going – they don't feel themselves subject to the laws of man and I don't remember them ever not getting away with it.

'If you don't believe me, think about this. An Italian-based, finance-oriented, autocratic, not to say dictatorial, male-dominated organization, with investments everywhere and huge political clout. What does that make you think of? The Catholics? What else?'

Jeremy swallowed. When he had thought about the Catholic Church, if he had thought at all, it had been of ornate buildings, priests in dusty robes, a negative attitude to most of the joys of life and parishioners confessing to impure thoughts. 'You seem to be hinting at a Mafia connection,' he said. 'But surely you're not serious.'

'I'm not suggesting a direct and open alliance,' Hazel said, 'although it wouldn't surprise me that much. But think about how many men must have business contacts with organized crime and still be devout members of the Church. Think how many Mafia members still go to confession.'

'Do they really?'

'Yes, they damn well do. When I was young, three gang members robbed a Catholic church in Boston. It took the church members about an hour to find out who they were and two more hours to find *where* they were. Nobody ever saw those three again. They may have been chased out of the state. Maybe not. Boston's a big harbour.

'I'll put it another way. You of all people should be able to look back in history. We're talking about the body which burned heretics at the stake and was in back of the Spanish Inquisition. Those of the world's truly evil deeds which were not committed in the name of patriotism were mostly carried out in the name of the Church. Can you believe that that body has changed in not so many generations into a bunch of hymn-singing powder-puffs? If you truly believe that, you'll believe me when I tell you that I'm a reincarnation of Joan of Arc. Am I getting through to you?'

Despite the heat of the sun, Jeremy gave a shiver. 'I'm beginning to get the picture.'

'And do you believe me?'

'You carry conviction. What, in your view, comes next?'

There was silence.

'Well?'

'We hadn't thought it all the way through, which isn't like us,' Hazel said. She went on slowly. 'My fault as much as yours. I'm just thinking it through now. It seems to me that the Church isn't going to cough up that sort of money to McKennerty without establishing provenance. The Grail itself, the German letter and the receipt might have been enough for a private buyer, but the Catholics are going to want to put it on show, like the Turin shroud, as a sacred object. They'll be less concerned whether such relics are genuine or are merely icons; the churches are full of fake relics of saints and they serve as objects for worship and therefore generate reverence and prayer. That's all that the Church asks of them.

'But as soon as such an object as the Grail surfaces, the debate has to be endless. That's all to the good, from the Church's viewpoint – argument is publicity and publicity keeps God in people's minds. Keep them arguing about that sort of issue and they forget to wonder whether there really is a God at all. On the other hand, there will be endless challenges from the devout and the sceptics alike. Think how the Shroud has been subjected to carbon-dating, microscopic and chemical analysis and every kind of non-destructive scientific test you can think of. Before they part with the hard-earned cash wrested from the faithful, they'll want to be pretty damn sure that it's bullet-proof.'

'Can our Grail stand up to that sort of scrutiny?'

'Probably. But that isn't the *point*. Their first step will be to establish provenance. We are the missing link in the chain. The German letter fills in a gap in the history as far as its arrival at Tinnisbeck Castle, back when the castle was known as Tynebrook. Before parting with a few million, the Church will want papers documenting its presence in the castle and its transfer to McKennerty.'

'There's the receipt.'

'The receipt I gave McKennerty was deliberately vague. It referred to the silver and the miniatures being *in a wooden box* and that's all. He thought that it was so that I could swindle my brother out of his share but really it was so that you could shout "Thief!" and prove that it was a forgery if that was how you decided to play it. Well, seems to me it's make-your-mind-up time again. If it helps, my name really is Hazel Carpenter now and if McKennerty thought I was your sister and not your wife he had wax in his ears.'

They sat in silence. The water burbled and another songbird was twittering away in the oak tree, but Jeremy only wished that they would shut up and let him think. 'Round about now,' he said at last, 'McKennerty and, if you're right, some very tough cookies representing the Vatican are probably telephoning and beating on the castle door, wanting answers to two questions. One – is it genuine? And – two – does McKennerty have good title to it?'

'Yep. Those are the questions. What will your answers be?'

'To question one, I don't know. To question two, same answer. I think we'd better go back to the *auberge* and phone Ian Argyll. If we really are much in demand, my first impulse will be to protract this very enjoyable honeymoon indefinitely and stay a long way away from home. But that would only be a confession that something was very far wrong and lead to a whole lot of just the sort of speculation we don't want. I think we'll have to go back and confront.'

'You may also have the police on the doorstep, wanting to know whether it was really stolen.'

'Question three. Same answer.'

They made themselves respectable, gathered up their trappings and climbed a bank to where the Porsche was waiting in the shade. 'Oh well,' Hazel said. 'It's been a good sort of honeymoon. Best I ever had.'

'I'll go along with that. And I'll tell you something else. I still get a kick out of this car.'

'The bride's present to the groom.'

'You already gave me a gold lighter.'

'For the small cigar you very rarely smoke. It was the best I could think of on the spur of the moment. This is much better.'

Mr and Mrs Carpenter neared home in the late afternoon, two days later. The northern air looked sharp and clear and felt cool after the heat of France.

The joiner's shop was deserted. They found Ian alone and restocking the bar in the pub. His face split into a wide grin when he saw them. 'Welcome back!' The grin faded. 'We were all sorry to hear about the old man. It had been coming for a long while, but it's hard when it comes. You'll miss him.' The grin made a shy return. His eyes found Hazel's rings. 'It's true what you said on the phone, then? Why could you not have been married from the castle and given us the excuse for a party? Were you not wanting to provide the drinks?'

'We thought that you could do with the business,' Jeremy said. 'Don't tell me that you didn't have a wee celebration.' Hazel was amused to note a return of the faint Scottish accent which had been absent while they were abroad.

'We had a bit of a *ceilidh* last night, sure enough. Some of the heads are sore the day. What will you take? It's on the house.'

Jeremy said that he could manage a small dram and Hazel agreed to join him. Ian poured malt whisky into three glasses. The two which he pushed across the counter were at least doubles. They toasted each other with the traditional '*Sláinte!*'

'Most nights,' Ian said, 'one of us has been sleeping in the castle, the way you said; or, if we couldn't manage that, we left a light on. And I've fitted the security locks you wanted on the doors and windows. Here are the keys.'

'Thanks.' Jeremy gave Hazel one set of keys and dropped the other into his pocket. 'Give me the bill when you've made it up.'

'Did you think I wouldn't? We've kept the place aired. There's been nobody else inside, that I'm certain of – they'd need a battering-ram to get inside now. I wouldn't know about phone calls. I saw you'd left your answering doodad switched off so we left it the same way. We've been getting phone calls most days, asking if you're back.'

'But has anyone been here looking for us?'

'There's been cars at the door. And that mannie who had the grey Porsche was here, asking for you. We said that you were away and we didn't know where. If anyone asks, do I say that you're back?'

'I'm afraid so,' Jeremy said. 'Let me know afterwards.'

'Surely.' Ian hesitated. 'I'm sorry about your granddad,' he said again, 'even if he was gey old. A fine man. Will there be a service?'

'No. He didn't want what he called "fuss and nonsense".'

Ian nodded. 'That sounds just like the man.'

They finished their drinks and prepared to leave. Hazel said, 'You can tell friends that there will be a party at the castle one of these days, to remember

193

the old laird and to celebrate our marriage, but not just yet.'

When the Porsche was on the move again, Jeremy said, 'That assumes that we can get through the next few days without being attacked or arrested.'

'It'll give them an incentive to keep us safe,' Hazel retorted.

The castle had become unfamiliar, like an old friend freshly met. The feel and smell were different. They made room in an outbuilding – supporting a stack of half-empty paint tins, Hazel discovered the remains of a seventeenth-century glass-fronted cabinet which only needed repolishing, most of the glass and the missing shelves replaced – and locked the Porsche away before they even busied themselves with unpacking and preparing a meal. They had stopped near Carlisle for some basic shopping.

Travelling had been the usual exhausting blend of discomfort, effort and boredom. They cut the evening shorter than usual and were preparing for bed when the cordless phone began its plaintive, ramped ringing. Jeremy took the call, sitting on the bed. Ian was on the line.

Jeremy had some difficulty interpreting the message. He was distracted. Now that she was properly married, Hazel had overcome her inhibitions about being seen partially clad; and the groom's presents to the bride had included some very fetching confections of silk and lace to add to the few items purchased in Edinburgh. 'Three?' Jeremy repeated vaguely. Hazel vanished into the bathroom and he pulled himself together. 'Did they say who was calling?' he asked.

The call finished. 'There have been three enquiries

about us,' he called. 'Each time, they were asked who was calling and they gave an evasive answer. "A friend." "They wouldn't know my name." That sort of thing.'

Hazel emerged. 'Three? That doesn't add up.'

'I'm afraid it does,' Jeremy said unhappily. The sudden injection of glamour was doing nothing for him. 'You go to bed. I have to do some thinking and make some preparations.'

'Can't I stay and help you think?'

'Please do, but put some clothes on,' Jeremy said. 'I can't possibly think while you're like that.'

'I'll take that as a compliment. I'd be worried if you could.'

The expected visitors arrived in the morning.

Jeremy had been down to the village, ostensibly for milk but more because the thrill of driving the Porsche was not yet fully satisfied. Over breakfast, they listened to the radio. The purchase of the Grail by the Vatican, it seemed, had not yet been completed, but venues where it might be displayed were already under discussion. The bulletin had descended into uninformed speculation when they were disturbed by the sound of a vehicle. From the kitchen window they could see that the large Japanese four-by-four which had brought McKennerty to the bank had arrived and was being parked near the Porsche.

Jeremy glanced at his wife. Her face was drawn and pale. 'You can leave this to me, if you like,' he said.

She shook her head. 'I'll do it. You can back me up, just the way we said. I'd be no use as backup to you.' She walked firmly into the hall.

Jeremy put a thick envelope into his pocket and took down his shotgun from a high shelf of the dresser. He already had cartridges in his opposite pocket. He left the castle by the back door, dropped quickly into the dip beyond the gravel and crawled quickly round the dead ground until he arrived almost under the wheels of the four-by-four. Looking through beneath the vehicle, he could see several pairs of male legs and his wife standing proud against the front door. Her voice came clearly.

'I do not intend to sign anything more,' she said.

Gordon McKennerty was confronting her, some papers on a clipboard in his hand. Two other men were standing nearby. Their attitudes were elaborately casual but the picture was one of menace.

McKennerty had returned to his domineering manner but he was trying persuasion, the iron fist in the velvet glove. 'Be reasonable,' he said. 'I paid you a hell of a price for that box of antiques, but the receipt you gave me was so vague it's useless. I'm only trying to complete the provenance.'

'Of the miniatures?'

'Yes, of course, of the miniatures.'

Confident that the men all had their backs to him, Jeremy rose slowly behind the big vehicle. He was startled to see a fourth man, whose feet had been hidden from him by the back wheel, leaning against the vehicle's side, a few feet away. Unseen by the men, Jeremy straightened for a moment and then lowered his head to look through the car's windows. He knew that Hazel had seen him and taken courage.

'You're a bloody liar,' she said. 'Those miniatures

are crap and you know it. It was the Grail you were after, all along.'

Jeremy saw the man's back stiffen. His very clothes seemed to bristle. 'I suppose the penny was bound to drop in the end, with all the publicity. Well, all's fair in business and you did bloody well out of it. All I want is a signature to a letter, stating that the box had been in your cellar here, unrecognized, for as long as you can remember.'

'You don't get it. It wouldn't be true. I made that box.'

McKennerty froze. Jeremy had the impression that the other men were waiting, secretly amused and expectant. McKennerty would be easy to obey but impossible to love.

'I don't believe it.' There was a pause while McKennerty thought it out. A tic beside his eye betrayed the strain he was under, but he was a quick thinker. 'Even if that was true,' he said, 'it doesn't matter. Scientifically, it tested out. All it needs is the provenance connected up. Sign the letter.' His tone was one of command and of absolute certainty that he command would be obeyed because he was who he was.

'No.'

So authority was not going to work. He became more pacific. 'If it's money you're after, would another ten K change your mind?'

Hazel hesitated for a moment, but hatred triumphed. 'No.'

Arrogance returned. 'Right. You've asked for it.'

McKennerty and one of the men – the man named Bruce – moved towards her. Bruce seemed to have recovered from his injuries.

Jeremy decided that it was time to intervene. He stole a quick look around. A flash of light from the far end of the drive caught his eye but he had no time to consider it. He raised his gun and fired one shot vertically into the air as he stepped out from behind the big vehicle, reloading as he moved. The echoes of the blast came back from the hills and seconds later the spent shot came pattering down around them. The men were frozen.

'Hold everything,' he said. 'You'll get nowhere by being violent. The sound of the shot will bring my friends up from the village. And I should warn you that the box and the miniatures were reported stolen immediately after your friends here came to visit in our absence.'

McKennerty had spun round, eyes narrowed. He recovered quickly. 'Who the hell are you? I paid Miss Carpenter good money for that box.'

'Don't you recognize me without my beard? I'm Jeremy Carpenter. And this lady isn't Miss Carpenter, she's my wife.'

'Carpenter?' McKennerty glared at him for a few seconds. 'I remember you. I bought your bronze.'

'Misleading me about its true value.'

'Is that what this is about? A con, in revenge?'

'For that and . . . other things.' Jeremy remembered in time that mention of Glynis might not be politic. It was quite possible that she had delayed her departure.

The exchange had absorbed his attention. He had forgotten about the man leaning against the car. The sudden alarm on Hazel's face alerted him, but too late. A hand came round his neck from behind and he lost some skin as the gun was plucked out of his fingers. The safety-catch had automatically been reapplied as he closed the gun or it would have fired again.

'We can do without guns, thank you,' McKennerty said.

The man was strong – too strong to know his own strength. Jeremy could see the world turning dark and knew that he could easily be killed, quite unintentionally, by the dangerous grip on his neck. In the desperation of the moment and to save his own life he could think of only one tactic for defence. He used his dwindling effort to grab behind him, find, seize and jerk.

The manoeuvre achieved all that he had hoped for. The grip on his neck vanished. The man screamed – there was no other word for it. He was doubled over. To make assurance doubly sure, as his strength returned Jeremy joined his two hands and brought them down on the back of the man's neck. His opponent subsided, face first. An upper denture bearing three front teeth skittered away across the gravel.

The shotgun had somehow been thrown clear and had impaled itself, muzzles down, in soft earth. Until it was rodded through, it would be a greater danger to a handler than to anyone else. So much for that.

Hazel was cursing shrilly. During the few seconds while Jeremy was distracted, there had been other changes. Bruce was gripping Hazel from behind and a knife-blade in McKennerty's hand was shining, mirror-bright, beside her face. A threat to slice her face would have been enough, but McKennerty was in a mood for overkill. He looked at his third henchman. 'Take him, Jimmy,' he snapped.

Jeremy had been lucky once but, although his blood

was up, he knew that he was no match for these burly and experienced toughs. There was no weapon readily available except his fists. He had read or heard somewhere that a fist is more effective while gripping something, even a box of matches. He dived into his pocket and came across the lighter. Hazel's gift might have a more useful function than for lighting the occasional small cigar. It was not as heavy as he would have liked, but clenching around it made his right fist feel more formidable.

The man came with a rush, grinning, while contemptuously ignoring the two blows which hurt Jeremy's fists more than his bullet head. Then the two were locked together. Jeremy back-pedalled, nearly tripped on his earlier enemy and slammed backwards into the side of the four-by-four. He was trapped in a bear-hug which was squeezing the breath out of him. He fought to win a little space so that he could bring his knee up. In the attempt, he braced his fists against the other's chin and pushed with all his might.

The move was much more effective than he could ever have expected. The lighter was still clenched in his fist and during his exertions the adjustment had been maximized. Under pressure, the piezoelectric ignition fired and the little flame roared, straight up the other man's nostril. The grip was broken immediately. The man – Jimmy – squealed and span away, tears hopping down his cheeks.

Hazel was held in a waist-hold from behind which had also trapped her arms. McKennerty was still holding the knife close to her face. 'You may not be so fucking brave while we have your wife with us for a hostage,' he said. 'Don't interfere or I'll start cutting.'

'If you make one mark on her,' Jeremy said slowly, 'I shall kill you as painfully as I can manage.'

The threat was empty and he knew it, but coming on top of his two victories – outrageous flukes, but only he knew it – it made the others pause. McKennerty was distracted and, while his eyes were on Jeremy, Hazel, her fury at detonation level, was given her chance. She fastened her teeth into his wrist and bit down with all the strength in her jaw. McKennerty screamed. The knife clattered down onto the gravel. Releasing McKennerty's wrist, Hazel tried to kick the knife away.

She had turned into a squirming, writhing, hissing tigress. There was blood on her chin. The man holding her was intimidated enough to relax very slightly his grip. She managed to turn partway. Her arms were still trapped and her heels seemed to be making little impression on the man's shins, but her teeth had proved effective once. She strained for the man's throat. He whimpered and reared back.

McKennerty was stooping to pick up the knife with his undamaged hand. Jeremy dived forward through a red haze of anger, determined to kick him over the castle keep and then pull the arms off Hazel's captor. He was delayed for a moment as the man Jimmy reeled blindly across his path, eyes and nose streaming. That gave McKennerty time to reach the knife. Jeremy steeled himself again for action. Somebody was going to get hurt.

The incipient bloodbath was aborted. A second shotgun blast woke the echoes and froze the contestants in their tracks – all but Hazel, who, finding her captor's grip relaxing, managed to get a grip on his ear with her teeth.

*   *   *

During the fracas, a black limousine had approached unnoticed along the driveway. There had been a time when all cars were black, but now black cars had become a rarity. To the film-makers, the black car was sinister. In real life, it more often carried top persons about their businesses. Jeremy's mind zigzagged as he tried to fit this new component into the shifting scene.

The shot had been fired by a man who stood close to the corner of the castle, holding a pump-action shotgun as though he knew very well how to use it. The black limousine made its final approach and stopped close to the same corner. The driver got out, carrying a similar gun. He was a broad man, appearing muscular rather than fat, while the man who had fired the shot was muscular in a more athletic style, but they were similarly dressed in grey suits over grey poloneck jerseys and each wore a dark grey hat. Except for the collar it could have been a clerical uniform.

McKennerty had straightened up without the knife. He was hissing between his teeth and nursing his bleeding wrist. Jimmy had come to a halt, whimpering. Bruce had pushed Hazel violently away, sacrificing, Jeremy thought, a piece of earlobe, and was moaning to himself while dabbing at his lobe with a grubby handkerchief. The third henchman, still down on his knees, was moaning over his denture which had been trodden on in the scuffle. Otherwise, there was silence as the driver, without lowering his shotgun, respectfully opened the rear door of the limousine.

The man who emerged was taller and leaner than his companions and his complexion was pale where theirs was very slightly olive. He wore a suit of darker grey but with a clerical collar. His hair on his hatless head was a similar clerical grey. His face was beaked and hawklike and his manner was that of one accustomed to command – and to being obeyed. In his presence, McKennerty's arrogance seemed mere bluster.

'That is quite enough, gentlemen,' he said. Such was the power of his presence that even the sounds of pain were reduced. He had an accent, but so faint that Jeremy could not be sure which Latin country it represented. 'You three –' he pointed in turn to each of McKennerty's men, '– go and sit in the back of your car. My men will be watching.' He waited impassively until the order had been obeyed.

'And now, Mr McKennerty. These men were with me as bodyguards because I expected to be carrying an international treasure, but we followed you from Edinburgh because I was sure that all was not as it should be. Your answers to some of my questions were evasive and your completion of the provenance seemed unduly protracted. And it seems that I was right. I had asked you to obtain further details of the provenance of the Grail. This, I presume, is Mr Carpenter, the owner of this castle since the death of his grandfather. He is, I believe, a direct descendant of Gavain Heydring, the addressee of the letter; in which case, I can envisage no reason for this fracas unless you were demanding proof which he was not prepared to give you. That in turn suggests that the box was either stolen or a fake. Which is it? Well?'

McKennerty had brought the bleeding from his wrist under control. He looked smaller in the presence of the tall man and much of his arrogance seemed to have ebbed away. 'I recognized the Grail and I paid good money for it, but I didn't get a proper receipt; just a list referring to a box and details of its contents.'

'Because he didn't want me to know what he thought he was buying off us,' Jeremy said.

'Thought?' The tall man seemed neither surprised nor disturbed by the implication.

'It's a fake,' Jeremy said.

McKennerty's voice went up most of an octave in his consternation. 'That's nonsense,' he exclaimed. 'It's been subjected to every test you could think of.'

'Tested, except for the provenance,' Jeremy said. 'It's a fake all the same. My brilliant wife made it from a balk of very old cedar and I wrote the German letter. I was about to show Mr McKennerty photographs which I took during the processes. He had swindled me over the sale of a bronze statuette and I had decided that what was sauce for the goose was sauce for the gander. I never intended the ultimate purchaser to suffer.'

'He's just saying that,' McKennerty said desperately. 'It's an act of spite because I twice recognized something good and bought it from him at a price which delighted him at the time.'

The tall cleric held out his hand. 'Let me see the photographs, please.'

With some difficulty, Jeremy pulled the bulky envelope out of his pocket. He extracted the photographs and handed them over.

Ian's van arrived and jerked to a halt, slithering on the gravel. Jeremy, recovering his mental balance, thought that the scene was beginning to resemble the start of a motor rally. He walked across and stooped to the window. Ian's eye were popping. 'Thank you for coming,' Jeremy said, 'but everything seems to be under control now. I'll explain tonight.'

Ian nodded and found enough space to turn the van.

The big moment was going flat. Jeremy backed to the low wall and sat down. Hazel joined him. He put an arm round her and could feel her shaking. 'I think it's over now,' he whispered.

McKennerty had moved close to the tall cleric and they examined the photographs with matching concentration.

'That would seem to put the matter beyond dispute,' the priest said. 'Mr McKennerty, you will be paid the value of a good fake and not a penny more. And for that price, I would also require a document promising absolute and total confidentiality.'

McKennerty's face turned white and then flushed a dark red as it twisted with passion. The priest was sheltered from his wrath by the prospect of a deal, albeit at a reduced value. McKennerty's rage focused on Jeremy and Hazel.

As McKennerty approached, Jeremy got up and moved in front of Hazel. The two men stood almost nose to nose. 'You bugger!' McKennerty said. 'I'll have my money back or I'll take you to court.'

Jeremy still had the envelope in his hand. He tapped it on his other palm. His voice seemed determined to shake in reaction, but he forced it to remain steady. 'You can put both ideas out of your mind,' he said. 'Your first idea was to steal the Grail, to save paying for it. I have a copied videotape here of two of your men burgling the castle. They make it quite clear what they're looking for. They only refer to you as Gordon and as Mister Mac, or the police, who have another copy of the videotape, would have arrested you by now. I have the original. I suggest that you go home and take a look at this one and at the copy of my statement to the police. You'll see that it would only take a whisper of your name and the proof would be staring them in the face. I'll make damned sure that plenty of people know the facts, but they'll say nothing unless you give me more grief. The receipt that my wife gave you is useless to you. It was typed on a machine a long way from here and signed with her name by somebody else. You understand?'

McKennerty made no answer. He stared Jeremy in the eye for a long moment. Then he snatched the envelope out of Jeremy's hand, turned away. He took a long, last look at the Porsche.

'Don't even think of it,' Jeremy said.

McKennerty glanced at the two armed men, then walked to the four-by-four. One minute later, the car was vanishing down the drive.

Jeremy remained on his feet. The priest spoke softly to him from ten paces away but his words were perfectly clear. 'From you, Mr and Mrs Carpenter, I require all your photographs, another signature and another promise of confidentiality. For this, a further payment can be negotiated. The authenticity of the Grail must not ever be disproved.'

'I don't understand,' Jeremy said. 'The thing is a fake. Its authenticity will certainly be disputed.'

The cleric shrugged expressively. 'But of course. There are always sceptics. As long as they can prove nothing, it does not matter. The value of any relic lies not in what it is but in what the devout believe it to be. It serves as a focus for their devotion. As to your motives in producing such a fake, I say nothing. The unpleasant

Mr McKennerty's reputation had been brought to my attention.'

Hazel stirred. 'Told you so,' she whispered. Louder, she said, 'He'd been abusing his wife and child in ways which even the Inquisition would not have tolerated,' she said. 'Half of his money went to them, to enable them to make a new life.'

The cleric smiled gently. 'Then I absolve you,' he said. He sketched what might have been a sign of the cross.

Twelve

Jeremy had been unaware of pain but once the action was over he began to nurse bruises. Hazel also was sore around the ribs. She thought that her mouth must be injured but concluded that the blood she spat out was not her own. As soon as they had arrived at a tentative agreement with the cleric and seen his limousine wafting imperturbably away over the bumps in the driveway, they hobbled into the kitchen and collapsed into the Windsor chairs.

Hazel was more nervous than hurt. 'You think you've pulled McKennerty's teeth,' she said, 'but from what I know of his reputation, he always pays off a score. Always. No matter how long it takes.'

'We'll just have to stay on guard,' Jeremy said.

'You still don't understand. He's quite capable of hiring somebody to . . . arrange an accident or even a fatal illness.'

Jeremy's sore ribs made speaking into an added burden. He decided to kill the discussion tone dead. 'Maybe we should have what your military call a pre-emptive strike.'

'Now you're talking,' Hazel said. 'There's a poetic justice in using his own money to pay somebody to knock him off.'

'I was joking,' Jeremy told her.

'Well, I was quite serious. He could burn the place down.'

'Now you're going over the top,' Jeremy said. 'Besides, if the Earl of Sussex couldn't do it, McKennerty can't.'

Hazel resumed her work on the damaged and laid-aside antiques in the cellar, but Jeremy was concentrating on clearing up his grandfather's affairs. These had already been in his hands for several years, so the process was simple. It left him plenty of time for his own worry. If some policeman made the connection between Gordon, Mr Mac, and McKennerty, or if some of the silverware included with the Grail were to surface, he would have to admit making a false report to the police. The alternative, continuing to argue that the goods had been stolen, would soon become perjury. Moreover, the true facts were known to a pillar of the Roman Catholic Church, whose silence might or might not be bought by a threat to reveal the true story of the Grail.

They were left to sweat it out for ten days, during which Jeremy imagined and discarded ever more improbable lines of escape. His swollen jaw returned almost to normal, a black eye faded and his ribs stopped hurting him. Life would have been good but for the black cloud of apprehension which seemed to blot out the sunshine and knot his stomach.

The return of Sergeant Carroway came to Jeremy almost as a relief. At least there might be a resolution, one way or the other. The Sergeant, bustling as ever, arrived in mid-afternoon and brought with him a small cardboard box. He nodded appreciatively at the new security locks. They led him into the kitchen and gave

Gerald Hammond

him a Windsor chair. The percolator was already at work and Hazel poured coffees. 'We Americans may not be good at tea,' she said, 'but we make good coffee.'

The Sergeant sampled his coffee and agreed politely. On the table, he opened his box and Jeremy recognized the miniatures and several pieces of silverware. His spirits sank.

Carefully, the Sergeant laid out the treasures on the table. 'I must ask you to look carefully at these,' he said. 'Are these some of the items which you reported as stolen?'

So far so good. They took their time studying them. 'Definitely,' Jeremy said at last.

'I agree,' said Hazel.

'We seem to have everything from your list except for one pepper-pot. I'll require a signature.' Sergeant Carroway produced from among several papers a detailed list. He hesitated, looking from one to the other, and pushed the list to Hazel. She accepted his pen. Before Jeremy could make a move to take over responsibility for the signature, she signed.

The Sergeant compared her signature with what was clearly a photocopy of the receipt she had given McKennerty. Jeremy felt acidity boil in his stomach. He was sure that he was developing an ulcer.

'If you get the items back, are you content to let the matter drop?' the Sergeant asked suddenly, putting away the papers.

'I don't understand,' Jeremy said faintly. He seemed to see a faint glimmer of hope. Breathing came more easily. Hazel, wide-eyed, was trying to make eye-contact.

210

The Sergeant half-smiled. 'Of course you don't. I'll explain. The court system has more than enough to cope with. The fiscals are not eager to prosecute, on disputable evidence, a man who is already facing a much more serious charge on evidence which looks rock-solid. And there would be little point spending a lot of public money and court time to obtain a sentence which would almost certainly be concurrent. So they've decided to drop this case. I hope you're agreeable.'

Jeremy would have been only too happy to agree but Hazel saw an opportunity to squeeze out a little more information. 'Not that anybody gives a damn whether we're agreeable or not?' she suggested.

The Sergeant looked hurt. 'That's not quite fair. The days have gone by when the victim was the last person to be considered. But, in this instance, there really is nothing to be gained. Present indications are that a prosecution for theft or resetting would not add ten seconds to an eventual sentence.'

'You mean,' Hazel said, 'that we were robbed by somebody who's done something much worse?' There was a pause. 'Of course, we're happy to get the family silver back, but I do think that you could tell us a little more,' she added, at what she thought was the psychological moment.

The Sergeant glanced at his watch. His shift would end shortly and he had no more visits to make. A rest from the continual driving was more than welcome. He was comfortable. His coffee was good and he enjoyed the rare privilege of restoring stolen goods to appreciative, rightful owners. 'I can tell you a little more,' he said. 'We've been kept informed, out here in the sticks, because this part of the case originated out

211

here. It wouldn't do for me to name names, but it will all be in the media in the next day or two anyway, so I'll tell you this much.

'The Edinburgh police have been keeping an eye on a certain gentleman. In that videotape that you gave me, there are several hints at his identity. He's a man of wealth and influence, so they had to be very sure before making any moves. The less said about his business dealings the better. He made enemies and several of those dropped out of sight. There was never any evidence of foul play and there was always some indication to the contrary – a postcard from abroad or a witness who claimed to have attended a farewell celebration at an airport.

'More recently, there was a report that two men had been seen bundling a woman into the back of a car. Well, that's not an uncommon occurrence during a family row. But there were other reports that this man's wife had also dropped out of sight. She seems to have had few friends, but two of the friends that she did have complained that she had failed to keep recurrent engagements. There were also reports from neighbours of unusual activity in the man's big garden, usually after dark. Also, two men had been seen around the place who answered the descriptions of the burglars in your video. That, plus some words overheard by the officers on observation, was enough for the granting of a search warrant. Your silverware and the miniatures were found in his house. He tried to bluff it out and produced a receipt which seemed to be from you, Mrs Carpenter, but, if there had been any question of its being genuine, the signature on it bears no resemblance to the one you gave me just now. However, the search mostly concentrated on the garden.'

'Don't tell me . . .' Hazel began.

The Sergeant nodded sombrely. 'It only took a day with sniffer dogs, probes and thermal-imaging cameras to begin turning up bodies. Six so far, I believe, although there may already have been more that I don't know about.'

The Sergeant finished his coffee, stretched and prepared to rise. 'One of them goes back years, I believe,' he said, 'but the latest, a woman, is very recent.

'That's all I know.'

Hazel seemed frozen. Jeremy got quickly to his feet and escorted the Sergeant to the door. 'You'll keep us informed?'

'Yes, of course.' The Sergeant touched his peak. Jeremy, after all, was a major landowner in the neighbourhood.

Jeremy returned to the kitchen. Hazel, very white, was swaying in her chair. She put her head down on her knees so that her voice came to him muffled. 'My God, Jeremy. What have we done?'

He began to rub her neck and shoulders. It was all that he could think of to try to calm her. 'We don't know that we did anything,' he said. 'If her husband . . .'

'Killed her.' Hazel sat up and shook his hands off. 'That's what you mean?'

'Yes. If he did. It may not have been anything to do with us. And she may have preferred it that way.'

'Nobody really prefers it that way. Jeremy, that poor woman! And the boy. He'll have to be looked after. We'll have to tell the police.'

Jeremy could foresee troubles ahead, stretching to

infinity. 'This needs sleeping on,' he said. 'Leave it until morning and we'll talk about it.'

'There's nothing to talk about. The authorities have to know that Glynis is dead and her husband's in prison and the boy has to be taken care of.'

'The home won't turn him out onto the street tomorrow.'

They left it there but all evening the subject hung in the air between them. In the morning, Hazel remained adamant. Whatever the cost, the authorities must be informed. 'If you don't,' she said, 'I will.'

Jeremy looked at her set face and could see that she meant it. He sighed. It could have been so good. 'You'd better let me do it,' he said.

The mobile phone was still in his pocket. It had proved useful and he had never seen the need to discard it as he had told Glynis to do. Suddenly, it produced its double tone. He flipped it open.

'Jason?' said the voice. 'I see that the bastard's been arrested. Do you think it's safe for me to go home now?'